Lock Down Publications and Ca$h
Presents

I0680403

LAND OF DA

HOOLIGANZ

PART 2

Written By
IRA B

Copyright © 2024 IRA B
LAND OF THE HOOLIGANZ 2

All rights reserved. No part of this book may be reproduced in any form or by electronic or mechanical means, including information storage and retrieval systems without permission in writing from the publisher, except by a reviewer who may quote brief passages in review.

First Edition 2024

Printed in the United States of America

This is a work of fiction. Names, characters, places, and incidents either are products of the author's imagination or are used fictitiously. Any similarity to actual events or locales or persons, living or dead, is entirely coincidental.

Lock Down Publications
P.O. Box 944
Stockbridge, GA 30281
www.lockdownpublications.com

Like our page on Facebook: Lock Down Publications
www.facebook.com/lockdownpublications.ldp

Stay Connected with Us!

Text **LOCKDOWN** to 22828 to stay up-to-date with new releases, sneak peaks, contests and more…

Like our page on Facebook:
Lock Down Publications

Join Lock Down Publications/The New Era Reading Group

Visit our website:
www.lockdownpublications.com

Follow us on Instagram:
Lock Down Publications

Email Us: We want to hear from you!

ACKNOWLEDGMENTS

First and foremost, I would like to thank God for blessing me with this fiyah ass pen game and creating a financial avenue to help me provide for my family. My mother, Mama BJ, my brothers and my nigga, Tyree, much love and appreciation for just being you and keeping it real.

Thank you to the big homie, Walt Holmes, hold your head up behind that wall. You always inspired me to take my intellect to the next level. I am also deeply indebted to my Quincey, Florida community for allowing me to experience the thing you've offered my life to create my stories.

I must point out that without the friendship and acceptance of LDP CEO CA$H, Bernice Burgos, Publicist Chanel Green, Kwame, "Dutch" Teague, Mellow Rackz and @Taytatted this would have been a very difficult mission to complete. My experience with them was one of the most gratifying of my life and changed me in profound ways. I think I finally understand the idea of love and loyalty, without that almost nothing else is possible.

And lastly, I want to say thank you to my faith and patience for always staying strong against the trials my current position, behind the wall, has brought my way. I'm a battle test and evolving by the day into further greatness.

DEDICATION

I dedicate this book to my nieces: Des Jazz, Kala, Diamond, Shay, Bug, Sassy and my beautiful Niya & Ky. I love you all with everything I have in me. Stay focused. And Jhene, I almost forgot you, but you will always be in that special place in my heart.

Chapter 1

The house was as quiet as a dead confidential informant found in a ditch with a bullet in his brain. But the pain and agony nagging in Heaven's heart for the loss of her brothers was the loudest silence within her tears. She was scared and alone, left with the burdens of her cold reality.

Just when she thought everything was over between the war with Lyonell and her crew, the FEDS swooped in and took everything that mattered the most to her. They took her brothers. They took Dejah. Why they didn't take her too, she had no clue, but one thing was for damn sure, she wouldn't give them the opportunity to do it again.

Heaven knew she had to step up to the plate or else lose her own self to the pressures of the universe. Her team was counting on her to hold the fort down. Her brothers needed her to be brave and ruthless in spite of their downfall for such characteristics.

It was her turn to finally rule now.

Queen of the Hooliganz, which meant that there was no space for weakness, which also meant her tears had to go. But she couldn't help it, Heaven just needed to get it out of her system. For three days, since the abduction of her whole team by the FEDS, all she did was cry in her silence. Up until the moment when her grief was interrupted by someone banging on her front door, like they were the police.

Instinctively, Heaven reached beneath the pillow on her bed and pulled from it a chrome Glock .19 that Shamar had recently gifted her. She then climbed out of bed and made her way to the front door. En route, she switched off the safety, in case there was cause to pull the trigger. Coming from where she came from and seeing what she saw in the trenches, Heaven knew better than to hesitate. Hesitation will get you killed. And she damn sure wasn't ready to die just yet.

At the door, Heaven peered out the side window curtain to see who was outside. When she saw who it was, a gasp escaped from her. Then she hurriedly reached to unlock the door, snatching it open at once.

"Hev," cried Toby the instant the door was swung open and she stepped inside.

"Oh shit, Toby!" Heaven tossed her arms around her. Of all the people she didn't expect to survive the fall from grace, it was Toby, who was standing before her eyes. "I thought you was taken along wit' the others," she said.

"I guess I was too swift for them muthafuckas. But I'm here, though, so what's the plan?"

"The plan? What is the plan?" Heaven shot her a puzzled look.

Then Toby returned that look with a stern one of her own. With the shake of her head, Toby walked away from her and went into the living room to sit down. Heaven locked the front door and followed Toby into the room.

"They didn't get everybody, Hev," said Toby. "White Boy Ty, Skoot, Durk, Pee Wee, they got ghost before the Feds could get them. So they're still out there somewhere. Those are the ones that's not accounted for, sis."

"But everybody else has gone to jail?"

Toby nodded.

The reality of it all seemed to have knocked the breath out of Heaven to the point she had to sit down. The burden was getting heavier and heavier by the minute.

"And you know what this means, right?" Toby spoke up, breaking the silence between them.

"What does it mean?"

"You are the last one left, Hev, the last of the original leaders of the HCG crew. I understand Delani, Shamar, and all the others were more prioritized wit' running the whole operation, but you, Heaven you have to step up now and carry the weight. You're the last piece on the board, the Queen. Only you can save what's left of the legacy, and I'm willin' to bet my life on it that your brothaz are feelin' the same way," said Toby with confidence.

"But how do they expect me to do this shit by myself, Toby?" said Heaven stressfully.

"Who said anything about you being by yourself?"

Heaven looked at her long and hard.

"But in order to survive at this stage, Hev, you have to understand you have everything to lose, if you make the wrong move."

"I know."

"Which means you have to move smart now, calculate your every step, and be goddamn ruthless."

"Ruthless?" Heaven whispered.

"Hell yeah," said Toby. "You gotta be ruthless in this high game, baby girl, there's no room for pity out there in them streets. You will be tested harder than ever now. Niggaz are gonna look at your young ass and believe you aren't built for the position you've been given, so you're gonna either show no mercy or die. Period."

Hearing those words, Heaven knew there was no way to go by doing it.

It was a very cold world out there, thought Heaven, as she dwelled over the matter at hand, very cold indeed.

Looking down at the gun in her hand and feeling the cold steel of its essence, Heaven wasn't afraid of the power in which it held over people's lives. She had her own power, too, the power of her own intelligence, knowing nothing could stop her, if she used it correctly.

"You can do it, Hev," Toby encouraged her. "I know you can."

"I can do it," said Heaven.

"Damn right, you can!"

Heaven nodded briefly.

"A'ight then," she said. "Let's get to it."

At that moment, she decided to do whatever it takes to prove to the streets that the crown was hers for the taking. She was about to change the game, at all costs.

Chapter 2

What was left of the HCG crew were all occupying the spaces available inside the Leon County Federal Detention holding facility, and even the county's Juvenile detention Center, for those that were not of age. A total of fifty-four of them, all affiliates of the Hooliganz Crime Gang, including several others, who had nothing to do with their street business at all. The FEDS claimed the HCG organization was one of the deadliest organized crime gangs of young rebels the south had ever seen. It was said they were into money laundering, extortion, murder, and kidnapping. Plus, they were entrepreneurs and well-respected in their community, because they always gave back, and did so without complaints. Kahlil, Delani and LJ were considered the top three commanders in the HCG crew, but little did they know.

For the past several days, the federal officials had been working strenuously to separate the crew, as much as possible. They wanted those with most influence to be separated from the others, because since their arrival, the HCG crew had been a constant problem. Violence was the answer to whatever came their way. From attacking officials and brutalizing other inmates, the HCG crew was a force to be reckoned with, and there was no stopping them, until they got what they wanted.

Things had gotten so bad that the warden over the federal holding facility had to bring Delani, Khalil and LJ together in an attempt to get them to bring peace to their crew.

"This what the fuck you crackaz wanted, so we gon' tear this bitch down," said Delani to the warden before hawking up cold and spitting in the white man's face.

That was Kahlil's cue to charge the warden and drive his head into his chin, knocking him down and out cold. It was the most he could do, being handcuffed behind his back and not able to do what he really wanted to do.

The five officials that were present went in for the kill, striking them with their fists, service radios, and then the Tasers came out. LJ was the first to be tased, which set Kahlil off, and he got his next. But somehow Delani had managed to slip off his cuffs, which got him a few good punches in before he was put down, too.

Sometime afterwards, the rest of the HCG crew found out what went down, and they tore that muthafucker up, like a bunch of young, wild hyenas on the loose.

And that's what the Feds had to go through on an everyday basis, until they were forced to shut the compound down. The HCG was compromised with and brought together as a whole, in order for them to cease their disruptive behavior. It didn't take the administration long to find the solution needed to find common ground with the crew.

The HCG was still running shit.

Their respect was earned.

Even when the interrogation episodes began, none of the crew's members had anything to say.

"You bitch ass crackaz can go eat a dick if you think I'll tell you anything," Wank Wank told them, when they tried to bitch him up with football numbers, if he didn't cooperate with them.

"We got two positive statements from a couple of your members, saying you're the chief of enforcers" said another

FBI agent to Shamar, who just laughed in their faces. "I see you think this shit is funny, huh," replied the white investigator, who resembled the actor Adam Sandler.

"You are very funny, Agent Bruce Carmichael, or should I say Big Head Hank Rogers from Holyfield Projects?" Shamar said, and watched the man before him reel back in his seat in sudden befuddlement. "Yeah. You thought I didn't who is you is? I wonder what Kim and the rest of the good people you've been betraying all this time would say to you and whatever you stand for, when they find out about who you really are. You may as well go ahead and kill yourself now."

The white man turned beet red in the face.

Shamar laughed at him. "And by the way," he said. "Big Head Hank, wasn't you the one that got caught fuckin' Tricky Shooby behind the pool hall? You need to go get yourself checked out, cracka, because you might not got long to live anyway."

"Get him the fuck out of here," agent Carmichael boomed.

Shamar was escorted out, laughing his ass off. When Shamar got back to the others, they laughed, too, at his antics.

The rest of the HCG crew stood firm and never budged, even the younger affiliates over at the juvenile detention center, where the Feds thought that they could break them into flipping one another. They thought wrong.

Dejah, who already knew their game and how it would play out, held strong and with unshakable faith, hoping that she would do as expected of her. It brought her heart peace to know that Redd was still out there in the trenches, where she belonged. Redd was seasoned, she knew what to do, so Dejah could sleep at night, knowing her loyalty was true.

Everybody was standing true, no weak links. Forever they vowed to remain loyal, no matter the circumstances. And that's exactly what they did, kept it real with their own.

And who would have ever thought Ced was actually FBI? The nigga had played his game so tight that it was hard to peep his game. And although the FEDS knew his death wasn't caused by the HCG's hands, but that of Lyonell's people, they were still trying to hold it over their heads because he was in their company when he bit the dust. Plus, Ced's wrath was his own fault because he shouldn't have been playing games from the get-go.

Another hard truth that Heaven had to deal with the loss of, and then the death of Marlon, whom the crew decided to not reveal the resurrection of. She had gone through enough heartache and Marlon's betrayal would only hurt her further.

They did it to protect her feelings.

But it was also believed that Marlon was probably the reason why Heaven wasn't locked up, along with the rest of them. And if that was true, then Marlon was one helluva nigga to convince the Feds to spare her, while she was just as devoted to the HCG crew as the rest of them. Whatever power that nigga had, he used it to the best of his ability to save his daughter.

Now it was Heaven's turn to do whatever it took to save her own daughter, Aliyah Renee. And also another hard pill for LJ to swallow, knowing that he probably would never be free again, to help raise their daughter together.

The same with Jamir and his girl, Harmoni, who was seven months pregnant with his child. The pressures of not being there for her were devastating, but Jamir was a tough shell to crack, and his faith in tomorrow was stronger than some.

They all were missing their loved ones, but they also accepted the fact that was what they signed up for, so there was no need to fall weak over them, now that they were gone. But they all still had each other, and that was all that mattered.

Their only hope was Heaven's survival now, knowing she would play her position accordingly. She would hold them down righteously. There was no breaking her.

Heaven was built just for this purpose, to stand firm against the odds. But only if they knew the hell that Heaven was about to create in the streets, in honor of her team.

Chapter 13

After their initial reunion, since the Feds came and ruined everything, it was just Heaven and Toby. Then, days later, Rikah came out of hiding, when she realized she still had some hope left. That hope was Heaven, and her chosen position as queen, now that Dejah was gone. When they saw that Rikah was still in the game, it gave Heaven and Toby more reason to believe that they could definitely capitalize together as a team.

While Heaven was the voice, Toby was the certified hustler, and Rikah, no doubt, was the muscle. Though the three of them together were fearless, individually, they would bust their guns, if it came down to it. And being that they knew and trusted one another already, there was no doubt that whatever they saw in their minds to do, it would get done thoroughly.

For the next week or so, the three of them worked together, cleaning up the mess their brothers left, assuring their families that they were safe and to count on them to take care everything. Heaven, who everybody knew was the new ruler of what was left of their team, was determined to champion her mission. But that was until she received that phone call from Red that changed everything.

"What did she want?" asked Toby. They were just leaving the Shaw Quarters neighborhood, after meeting up with a nigga named RJ, whom Bizzy said owed him some money.

They collected the seventy–five hundred and left RJ leaking from several orifices, hesitant to do it.

The first person that reached out to Heaven was Vermani, then the rest of the hooliganz, and from them requests were made, and Heaven saw to it that it was being done.

Heaven said, "She wanted to meet up with us. She said she got something for me."

"What she got?" asked Toby.

"I'm determined to find out right now." Heaven told Rikah to take them to the Tallahassee Mall, where Redd asked them to meet her at. Why she chose the mall, Heaven had no clue, especially after hearing the seriousness in Redd's voice in regards to what she said she had for her.

Twenty minutes later, they reached the mall and were directed to the Gucci store. That's where they found Redd, humbled as always, sitting down before the shoe section on a padded bench, trying a pair of sandals.

Both Toby and Rikah spread out about the store, but kept close to their queen and watched their perimeters attentively. Redd beckoned Heaven over to sit down next to her, and she did so without question.

"How are you holding up, love?" Redd asked. She had changed her whole identity, with the boyish Amber Rose look and a pair of green eyes that still shone of the beast that lied just beyond.

"I'm making it," said Heaven.

"It's a lot of heavy responsibility now, huh? Everybody is depending on you to keep the torch flame?"

Heaven nodded.

"Well consider yourself blessed, despite the circumstances you've been present with. But that's why I'm here, Hev, to assure you that no matter what the circumstances are, you got someone loyal and thorough standing by you," said Redd.

"No doubt," Heaven replied. "You have always been good to me, and I do appreciate you, Redd."

"I got something for you, love."

"Okay."

With the same brand new sandals on her pretty, red, pedicured feet, Redd stood up and asked Heaven to follow her. From there, she led the way to the back of the Gucci store and into the storage room area. Heaven entered the room behind her and moved her hand towards her waist line, where her pistol was hidden, just beneath her Fendi coat. She was ready, in case something shady was going on. In spite of her new position, and the awaiting vibes that would be coming her way, Heaven wasn't doing no slipping. No matter who she was in the company of, she was determined to survive.

A minute after, Redd led her to a section of the room, where big duffle bags sat upon the floor. Heaven stopped and stared down at the bags, then when she looked over at Redd and there was a grin on her face.

"What's in the bags, Redd? What's so damn funny?" replied Heaven suspiciously, and with seriousness.

"That," Redd gestured towards the bags, "is your new beginning, Hev. All four of those bags contain a total of six point two million dollars in cold, hard cash. Dejah's blessing to you to give your new position the push that you need to prosper in this game."

"Six million dollars, Redd?" Heaven gasped.

"And it's all yours."

All Heaven could do was shake her head.

"And before you allow your mind to wonder why I didn't just take the money for myself and run with it, let me remind you of something. I am loyal to my woman, Dejah, no matter how much money is involved. I'm only doing what she asked me to do. And besides, I know the money is in good hands now. You are Queen of the city now. The streets are yours. And to survive in them streets, you must have the three most important qualities: money, power, and respect." Redd replied, before Heaven asked her where would she be in the process. "Where else? Serving my new queen, until I figure out a way to get my woman back out here with us."

"I respect that," said Heaven. She still couldn't believe that Dejah had left her six million dollars in cash.

"So how do you plan on proceeding in this matter?" asked Redd.

Good question, thought Heaven.

Chapter 4

"I want five thousand to go on the books of every last one of our hooliganz," said Heaven to Rikah. "That's your job for now, so get to counting."

Also present in the house was Redd, Toby, Heaven's mother, Monica, Harmoni, and Shamar's wifey, Danielle. It was clear that Heaven was calling the shots now, and there was no question of her authority. Even Monica didn't question her daughter's demands, for she understood the powers that be and knew the importance of her position.

"Next, Toby, we need to assemble a solid team. I want numbers, all females. You know the qualities that's needed to make the cut. If I see anything other than what we need to secure a solid team, I will kill them, and then I will deal with you accordingly, myself. Understood?" Heaven looked over at Toby and Toby saluted her.

"It's understood, Hev. I gotcha," she replied.

"And mama? This house has to be replaced with something bigger, with heavy security. And please be discreet about it because no one outside of those in this room, or those we know worthy, should know where I'll be resting my head," said Heaven to her mother.

"What's the price range should I quote, baby?" Monica asked her daughter. Heaven had already made he quit her day job to stay at home and raise Aliyah Renee, while she ruled the streets that were in dire need of her presence, and whatever else she had to offer.

"Two million should do it for now," said Heaven. And thanks to Redd, she now had Dejah's drug connections. Once the time came, Heaven would make the necessary contacts and hand the mission over to Toby to orchestrate. Toby was the true hustler and the drug game would be her area of expertise to handle. Monica nodded her head and bounced to her feet to go see to her new task. She would call up Anya, and together, they were gonna find the best home to accommodate their daily life and satisfy their young queen.

The next order of things was for Danielle to go out and find the best lawyers money could buy for the representation of her team. Heaven wasn't playing when it came down to her crew, and by all means, she was willing to do whatever it took to get them back home to her.

Once all her bases were covered, and everybody was doing what was asked of them, Heaven took the time out to reflect on her predicament. She knew that the Feds were probably still out there watching, which was why she planned on remaining in the shadows. She would do better than what Dejah did, and her ultimate goal was to win at all costs. Like Toby and Redd had told her, she would have to be smarter and more ruthless than anybody who'd ever claimed her position. Heaven knew the dynamics of the game, she knew the importance of being a queen pin, but little did she know, though, despite what she knew, fate still had a plan for her.

Heaven was also a scholar, therefore she decided to resume her college education online, instead of attending her classes in person. But she did go out and purchase books on those who her new status was equivalent to, the king and queen pins of America, the ups and downs, their mistakes and all, including the lessons from those she'd witnessed with her own eyes. She wanted to learn what she needed to know to prevent making the same mistakes as those who came before her. She was devoted to the game and her people. She would use the knowledge she gathered from those before her versus the present matters she was faced with, and capitalize from there.

Heaven didn't have failure as an option.

She was sure of her position, the chosen one.

"I got a few solid bitches I did some time with who's about to get out soon who'll fit right in with what you got going on here," said Redd, some days later, when they were occupying Shamar's Horizons Bookstore and Lounge, where he had Danielle's aunt running the show.

"And they're capable of standing firm?"

"Two of them for sure," said Redd. "And the other one, Sheena, I didn't have long to really bond with her. But she has potential, Hev, and I believe she could be a great asset."

After dwelling over the matter for a minute, Heaven knew that she could count on Redd to make the wisest decision. But regardless of that assurance, Heaven still felt the need to warn her that she wasn't putting up with any bullshit.

"What's understood don't need to be explained," Redd said, before Heaven could even respond.

"Because they will die, Redd, no exceptions."

Redd nodded. "It's understood…"

With that being said, they promised to revisit the matter when the time came. Until then, Heaven proceeded with her mission to assess the group of females she had standing before her that Toby had recruited. There were nine of them to start with, three of them Heaven already knew of, and she was far from convinced that they were worthy to be part of her team.

"How many of you are strapped right now?" Heaven came to stand before them. This was the moment where she would have to make a vital statement and prove that she was fit for the position she was given.

All except two of the females had pulled out her weapons, both guns and knives, and to them Heaven nodded her approval.

"What's your name, Sweetheart?" Heaven asked one of the two who didn't present a weapon of any kind.

"Meesha," she said.

"Okay, Meesha, come with me." Heaven beckoned her with a wave, and Meesha stepped out of line to follow her.

Standing nearby Toby watched quietly as Heaven led Meesha over to the other female, who didn't produce a weapon. For some reason, her heart began thumping with adrenaline as she anticipated what was about to take place.

"And what's your name?" Heaven asked the female, who said her name was Ari. "I like that name. Ari," she said and turned back to Meesha. "What am I to you, Meesha?" replied Heaven gravely.

"The boss?" Meesha said, with a hint of uncertainty.

"And you, Ari. What am I to you?"

"My queen," said Ari.

That made Heaven smile. But that smile disappeared when she said, "That's right. I am your queen. And your queen is ordering you to kill Meesha with your bare hands, since you don't have a weapon to do it with."

"Huh?" Ari hesitated.

That's when Meesha struck and hit Ari with a two-piece combo to her face that made her stumble on her feet. Then she followed through with a lethal blow to Ari's windpipe, crushing it on impact. Ari reached for her neck, gasping for air and struggling to breathe.

"No mercy," Toby replied.

Without further ado, Meesha went in for the kill and snapped Ari's neck, killing her instantly. Ari dropped down to Meesha's feet and didn't move again.

"No mercy," Meesha turned to Heaven and said.

Heaven looked at her and saw the monster in her eyes. She like Meesha. The bitch was vicious.

"You did well, Meesha. Get back in line." Heaven refused to show her any further respect at the moment." Toby looked at Meesha and smirked.

"Welcome to Royal Mafia everybody," said Heaven. "We are Royal Mafia and making the wrong move, like you just witnessed, will get you killed. I am your queen and you are all queens, too. We're royalty, Royal Mafia. Toby?" Said Heaven to her most faithful.

"Yes, Hev?"

"Royal Mafia?" said Heaven.

"Royal Mafia," she replied firmly and sure.

Heaven nodded and said, "Make 'em respect that shit." Then she turned around and walked away from the group to go see about to the important business.

Rikah fell in stride and opened the door for her, and Heaven made her exit. Royal Mafia was now in effect. Either they were gonna get down with the team, or die in the process.

Chapter 5

The hooliganz were all outside, enjoying the fresh air and sunshine on threads. Surrounding them were dozens of other guys, doing their thing and discreetly watching the youngsters, wondering what they were up to. LJ, Delani, and some of the other hooliganz were utilizing their rec time, working out and trying to stay in shape. Delani was leading the workout session with core burning exercises.

"War ready at all times," said Skinny.

"For sho," added Jeremy, jumping back up to his feet after completing his round of burpees. Right then, Booby got down and began his set of burpees.

"Y'all heard anythang on the juniors?" asked Trill, referring to the younger hooliganz who were over at the juvenile detention center, giving them hell, too.

"I spoke wit' my old boy a coupla days ago," said Lil LuLu, whose cousin, Youngin, was one of the thirteen junior hooliganz over at "The Tent." He continued, "Youngin and 'nem were in there wildin' out like a muthafucker."

"Who's the most influential we got there?" Kahlil asked.

"Hollow and Bush Boy," said Shamar, and met the gaze of Delani, who looked at him in surprise that he didn't mention Jamir in that category.

It was then that LJ gave the order to a few of the hooliganz to contact their people in regards to the junior situation. They wanted the younger hooliganz to give them hell over there, but someone of more influence needed to step up the plate and bring some type of structure to their group.

"What's up wit' Jay?" Kahlil asked Shamar. "You heard anything?"

"I talked to LaShonda, she went to see him yesterday. I'll know something when I talk to her later. But last I heard he was still pretty banged up and healing, though."

During the sneaky ambush from the Feds, Jamir had resisted arrest so aggressively that he ended up getting his arm broken, a couple of cracked ribs, and a tooth knocked out. Baby brother was going through a lot right now, on top of the fact that he left his girl and unborn child out there.

"We gotta figure out a way to get my juniors outta there," said Delani. "We need them back in the trenches, to carry on our legacy."

"What about us though?" said LuLu.

"We gon' be a'ight," said Vermani, while in the middle of doing the last of his push-ups.

Moments later, a group of seven older niggas approached the crew from across the yard. Chili Willie was the first to spot the movement and alerted the others. At once, the hooliganz got in position and reached for their shanks, readying themselves for whatever was coming their way.

"Ain't that's the nigga Sonic coming this way?" Wank Wank suddenly appeared at Kahlil's side.

"Yea," said Kahlil.

"Wonder what this nigga want."

"Everybody knew that Sonic was "the man" on the pound. He had major pull inside the gates. He was also affiliated with Crips and was said to have one of the highest ranks in his sect.

As they approached the hooliganz, all eyes were looking in their direction. It was a legend that when dealing with Sonic, someone is likely to die or get connected.

"If smoke he wants, then I'ma give 'em smoke," replied Trill, ready to put in some work.

"Just be on point," said Jeremy.

"Always," Kahlil nodded.

When Sonic and his crew finally made their way over to the hooliganz, it was Delani who stepped forward to be the voice of his people.

"What it do, fellaz."

Sonic was a stocky built, light skin nigga in his mid-thirties. When he spoke, it was obvious that his accent was derived from his island roots. "It take it y'all already know who I am," he said.

"Just state your business," said Delani.

Sonic smirked at his direct approach. "For starters, I respect you lil' niggaz movement and I've heard all about your situation out there in the streets. But my people speak very highly of you, and for that," said Sonic and nodded to the man at his left, who stepped forward with what appeared to be a bundle of something inside a leather pouch. "I'm making my offering to you outta respect and honor to you and your people."

When Buzzy moved to accept the offering, Kahlil stiff-armed him to keep his position.

"We good on that, big homie. Whatever me and my hooliganz need, we gon' get it ourselves," said Delani.

"And how are you gon' do that without going through me, first?" said Sonic, feeling some type of way about how he was being handled at that moment.

"Nigga, we don't need you to get this poppin'. You better go back and do your muthafuckin' homework. It's HCG on this side, and we don't need shit from you," sneered Delani.

"Like that shit means anything to me. This is my pound! Nobody moves unless I say so," snapped Sonic.

"You got three seconds to go back the way you came," Bizzy spoke up and drew his bone-crushers. One after the other, the rest of the hooliganz clutched their weapons and got into their battle stance.

Again, Sonic smirked and nodded gravely to Delani. "We'll see who's who eventually."

"We can get kraken' right now," suggested Vermani.

"Later," Sonic turned around and walked away.

"Later? Who this nigga take us for?" Kahlil replied and gave his hooliganz the signal. "Let's eat."

Without further ado, the hooliganz struck out against Sonic and his crew. There was no way they were gonna wait until later to get some straightening. It was either do or die right now, right then and there, and the hooliganz wasn't bowing down to no one.

But little did the hooliganz know, the seven of them was just a small fraction compared to who else was lying in wait for just that moment. Sonic had all types of niggas ready to move at his slightest whim. And before the hooliganz even realized what was goin' down, they had been surrounded and advanced upon, with murderous intent, by a whole nother force. That's when shit got real ugly.

It was a blood bath.

A massacre.

Chapter 6

During that same hour, Cassandra "Baby Gal" Dawkins pulled up to a stop at the curb outside her mother's house on Lee Road. Before climbing out of the smoke gray colored BMW M5 Sedan, Baby Gal reached across to the passenger seat where the shiny gift bag was. She retrieved the bag, peered inside and smiled to herself. Then she got out and headed for the front door of the house.

Ever since joining her Royal Mafia a few weeks ago, Baby Gal had been in her element. She had money now, a brand new BMW, and a loyal team she could now call her own.

Before then, Baby Gal was barely getting by, jacking petty hustlers for their work and boosting. Then Heaven came along and offered her the opportunity of a lifetime. With that commitment came a brand new car, a hundred dollars in cash, her choice of weaponry, and a force to be reckoned with by way of a sisterhood that vowed to have her back for better or for worse. Baby Gal had never felt so dedicated in her life. She was true to her shit, a real female goon in the flesh.

Baby Gal made her way to the door and let herself inside. At her entrance, she broke out in a wide grin when she found her mother, Sonya, sitting in her favorite chair, with her head on her chest, asleep. On the TV across from her head was a rerun of Family Feud. Steve Harvey, once again, was looking splendid in a tailored emerald green Tom Ford suit and snake-skin loafers.

"Wake up, sleepy-head," said Baby Gal in a whisper, before placing a kiss upon her mother's forehead.

Sonya's eyes fluttered open and she lifted her hand up to meet the sparkling gaze of her loving daughter. Then she cracked a smile and said, "You caught me."

"You got a little drool right there, too, at corner of your mouth," said Baby Gal and got her hand swiped away from touching her mother's face.

"Get away from me 'fore I kick you," Sonya replied, and then spotted the bag behind Baby Gal's back. She inquired about the bag, and it was handed to her, as her daughter perched upon the arm of the chair next to her.

"I was out shoppin' and I thought about you."

Inside the shiny gift bag was a Versace head scarf and a pair of earrings that sparkled with quality.

"I love it, Baby Gal. Thank you, sweetie!" Sonya beamed up at her daughter with genuine joyousness. Then she got up to go stand before the old vintage mirror on the wall by the long sofa chair. "These are beautiful," she said as she held the earrings up to her ears in front of the mirror.

"Glad you like them," said Baby Gal. "And where is that brotha of mine?" she asked.

At the mention of the sixteen year old brother, Corey, her mother frowned and turned around to face her. When Baby Gal saw the expression on her face, she automatically knew what she was about to hear wasn't good.

"What is it now, mama?" she asked. The last time she saw her little brother was a week ago, when she bumped into him in the convenience store. Then he smelled like a pound of weed and their communication was brief, before he had to go with his "homies."

"I don't know what that boy got going on out there, Baby Gal," Sonya shook her head sadly, and then she moved back over to reclaim her seat.

"When was the last time you saw him?"

"A coupla nights ago, when he came through that door wit' blood all on his clothes." She shook her head no. "He just kept on telling' me not to worry about it," said Sonya. Then she went on to tell Baby Gal about pressing Corey about the matter and walking in on him reloading a gun in his bedroom. She chastised him about bringing joints into her house, an argument ensued, and Corey packed a travel bag, left the house and never came back.

Having had enough, Baby Gal pulled out her smartphone and proceeded to call her little brother.

"He won't even answer when I call," said Sonya.

"I got it," Baby Gal told her.

When she was sent straight to voicemail, Baby Gal hung up and forwarded a text message to him.

Again, Sonya rose up out of her chair, and this time, exited the living room for the kitchen. Looking up at her mother's retreating figure, Baby Gal knew if she didn't do something about her it would burden their mother down.

After delivering the text message, Baby Gal then called her home-girl, Amanda. Their brothers, Todd and Corey, were the closest of cronies. When she made contact with Amanda, it was then that Baby Gal was given the lowdown.

"Oh you ain't heard, gurl?"

"Heard what?"

"Todd and Corey ain't tight like that no more," Amanda replied with earnest thickening her voice.

"Whatcha mean ain't tight no more? Them two niggaz been tight since the third grade."

"You think I don't know that, gurl? They been fell out weeks ago. Since Corey started hanging around his new crew, him and Todd don't even talk to each other."

"What new crew?" Baby Gal wanted to know. If what Amanda said was true, then Corey must be doing some serious business for him to break off his friendship with someone he'd known almost all his life.

Amanda didn't know exactly what crew Corey was out there hanging with, only that they're making a little name in the streets. All Baby Gal could think about was whether her brother was making the right moves or not.

If only she knew what her little brother was really up to out there.

"Ask Thomas Mitchell's boy." Sonya appeared in the kitchen doorway.

Baby Gal looked over at her mother quietly.

"That's who I'm hearing he's been associated wit' lately," she said, and Baby Gal felt her heart skip a beat.

Solomon "Solo" Mitchell was a name that had been circulating in the streets for years. He was a young killer, the one of a legendary gangster. Solo was bad business, and if this is who her little brother was cliqued up with, then Baby Gal had a whole lot to worry about.

Bad move.

Anybody but Solo Mitchell.

Chapter 7

Heaven didn't even look at her own two best friends the same anymore. Not because of who she was now, but because she knew they would never accept the fact that they didn't fit the criteria. She loved Veronica and Monique with everything she had in her, but Heaven would never subject them to what lie ahead for Royal Mafia.

She wanted killers on her team, vicious killers and strategic thinkers under pressure. That's what was needed in order for Royal Mafia to survive in this game.

So far, Heaven had made the proper contacts with Dejah's connect, and a backup connection of her own, in case they didn't see things her way. She put Toby in position to organize her own team of hustlers. They had four trap houses doing numbers with the new product. Toby and her team were distributing through the area.

Toby was doing her thing.

In the process, Heaven was expanding her empire and seeing to it that the Royal Mafia was standing on business and earning the rep that it deserved.

With Redd as her right hand bitch and Rikah as her closets and most valuable shooter, the Queen of Royal Mafia couldn't go wrong and was proud of what she'd accomplished. She had a total of sixteen crew members, and they all were hustling and proving their worth. So far they had minor problems within the crew, where two numbers didn't see eye to eye, and Heaven saw to it immediately that the matter got resolved.

Those same two crew members, Dyamond and KeKe, were made to pair up and work together on vital tasks, which would determine whether they were capable of being team players or not. Now the both of them were almost inseparable, having settled their differences and made the remainder of the crew out of believers.

KeKe and Dyamond were meant to be.

When you see one you saw the other, and if crossed, they would get on that ass together.

But those weren't the only ones who were making a great impression in the crew. There was Leekah, twenty years old and vicious as they come. She killed her first victim at the age of fifteen, while breaking into a house and getting caught by its owners. She stabbed the husband to death with his own kitchen knife, and left his wife severely injured. Since then, she'd murdered four other people.

Then you had Tap Tap, a young seventeen-year- old dyke bitch, who was accustomed to extorting niggas and robbing jewelry stores with her partner-in-crime, Lacey. Between them, they both had a half dozen bodies under their belts.

And one of Heaven's favorites, Gucci, a beautiful young redbone black sheep at the age of nineteen, was just as intelligent as she was deadly. She was one of them smartass silent killers, one who would poison your drink or catch you when you least expect it, like sitting behind you in the theater.

The rest of the crew were talented loyal goons, not perfect by a long shot, but likable enough to keep around. And because of them, the Royal Mafia had become an organization to be admired.

The streets already knew what it was. It was turning out to be a wonderful thing.

Heaven was doing quite well for herself.

It was happening. All the things that she doubted would happen were taking place right now. She was winning. She was prospering and content with it.

Then all that changed at the ring of Heaven's phone, as she distanced herself from the five star restaurant on North Monroe Street, where she had lunch with her friends. When she looked down at the phone and saw Kiara's number, something in her gave her pause. A premonition of something very heavy awakened inside of her.

"Hey, Mama Kay. What's up?" She replied humbly. And that's when Heaven heard the miserable cries of the women she'd grown to love like a mother.

"What's wrong?"

"He's dead," she sobbed. "They murdered my baby." Heaven heard those words and her heart squeezed with burning emotion

"Who's dead?"

Kiara cried even harder and then Heaven hard the sound of the phone dropping on the other end.

Next to her, behind the wheel, Brianna, who was Heaven's personal driver of the Rolls Royce Wraith that once was owned by Dejah, looked at Heaven and saw a very disturbing look in her eyes.

"Ma," Heaven yelled into the phone. Her heart was pounding so very hard in her chest that it left her breathless.

Moments later, the sound of Kiara's sorrowful, grief-stricken cries erupted in the background on the other end of the phone, and it was horrifying to hear.

Her scream scared Heaven deeply. There was only one reason why a mother would sound this way, the death of her child, or children, or that of a parent, and both of Kiara's parents were already dead and gone. So that left the twins, and she only referred to one of them being dead.

A tear escaped Heaven's eye at the thought of one of her brothers being dead.

Suddenly, someone else picked up the phone, and it was a man other than her husband that spoke up.

"Hello?"

"Who is this?" Heaven demanded.

"This is Sheldon Price. I'm Kiara's coworker. I think someone needs to come retrieve her," he replied.

"What's going on, Sheldon?"

"All I know is she just got a phone call about her son, Vermani."

"What?" Heaven cried. "Vee?" she sobbed loudly.

"I will stay with her until someone arrives. Kiara doesn't need to be alone right now and—" the conversation was cut short when the phone was suddenly flung into the windshield and broke into pieces upon impact. Heaven put her face in her hands and let out a loud powerful wail.

Vermani was dead.

His death would change everything.

Brianna looked for a place to pull over and Rikah, who was now busily on her own phone in the back, was silently crying, trying to focus past her tears.

When the car was parked on a side street off of Tennessee Street, between a convenience store and Wendy's, it was there that Brianna pulled her queen into her arms. They cried together and the only thing that mattered at the moment was each other. But when the tears dried, blood would be spilled, so much blood that you could swim in it.

Later, word got back from the prison that war had broken out, and seventeen people had died. None of them was from the HCG crew. They all were the opps, and two of them were prison guards. The hooliganz had taken a great loss today. Retaliation was a must.

"Y'all know what time it is," said Heaven, when she met up with her whole team in the evening. "It's time to let that monster out," she commanded.

All it took was one name in regards to who was responsible for initiating the war. And although Sonic was dead already, that still left his loved ones, and whoever else stood with him had to fall.

"Here we go again," said Rikah. She prepared herself for war, and to cause hell on earth, just like they did when Lyonell had come with the fuckery.

The streets were still stained with blood from the war, and now the temperature was up again.

Chapter 8

He was so distraught and devastated over his brother's death that Delani didn't feel the physical pain. He was still laid up in the infirmity, after enduring multiple stab wounds. He had a punctured lung and another vicious blow to the neck, missing his main artery by three inches. Several more to his back, chest, and leg, and Delani was still ready to get up and do it all again.

Every time he closed his eyes, he saw Vermani strewn on the ground, choking on his own blood. That image would never leave his mind. It would haunt all his tomorrows. For days now, since his two brothers' deaths, all Delani did was cry until he became so emotionally drained it put him to sleep. Then he'd wake up again and do the same thing. Jeremy was dead. Lil LuLu was gone. And Vergo died from a knife to the heart. Kahlil had put in work and laid three of them niggas out. Delani himself had bodied two of them fools, and severely damaged several others in the process. Even when the task force came in with tear gas, riot bean bag guns, and rubber bullets shotguns, the hooliganz were still making it count. Bizzy and Shamar had been hit with rubber bullets, but that didn't stop them, it only intensified the rage that was already surging through them.

Delani, who had never experienced the grief and anger that was burning within him, was ready to die now, too. He was gonna make them kill him in there. Killing his brother had forever awakened the demon in him. That demon would never rest now.

It was demon time.

He had overheard talk in the prison medical ward, concerning the deaths on the street deriving from what took place inside the prison gates. The killings has been all over the radio stations and news. From what little Denali gathered from numerous discussions he'd overheard throughout the ward, it was determined those who were being killed were not any of his people. But it was also hinted that those responsible were indeed affiliated with the Hooliganz Crime Gang. It had to be, if the only people who were dying out there were related to Sonic and to who he called his own.

Heaven, thought Delani. He knew it had to be her. She was pressing the buttons, making it happen.

Or maybe it was Big Los' people out there wrecking shit in his honor. Carlos "Big Los" McClendon was also from the Pepper Hill area of Quincy, which is where Delani and the initial members of the crew were from. When the war popped off on the yard, Big Los and his niggas intervened and put in work alongside the hooligans. He had lost a few of his people in the process, which was reason enough for his people to retaliate outside the prison gate, as well.

Either or, Delani was appreciative of their loyalty, but he was too distracted by his own pain inside to worry about things he couldn't control.

In the middle of his darkening through process, the door to his assigned medical ward observation cell opened and in walked Nurse Brown, with the prison guards. They entered the room and Delani sat up on his padded bunk, glaring past the nurse at the guard.

"It's okay, Delani. Don't fret, honey. I won't be long and I'll leave you be," said Nurse Ranajah Brown, a pretty, chubby, dark skin woman in her late twenties. Since his arrival back from the local medical hospital, it had been Nurse Brown, who had been taking good care of him.

Delani glared continually at the guard, who looked a little uneasy under his threatening gaze. Two other guards had been killed during the deadly showdown, and Delani knew there was a possibility that the rest of the guards would want to try some slick shit.

"Be cool," said Nurse Brown, placing a gentle hand upon his chest and applying a little pressure to get him to lay back down, so she could take his blood pressure.

After a few more attempts Delani, lay back down, but kept his eyes on the guard standing in the doorway.

"Somebody sends their love to you, too, Delani," whispered Nurse Brown, as she proceeded to check his vital signs.

He snatched his eyes away from the guard to look her dead in her eyes. "Who?"

"Shamar and Kahlil, and pretty much the rest of your boys. I just saw them all while doing my med rounds." This wasn't the first time Nurse Brown had brought him word from his brothers. She was cool, and definitely for the struggle. "They said for you to hold your head up and say solid."

"Let them niggaz know that I'm good."

"No you're not." She frowned at him. "I see your eyes, you've been crying again."

"I can't stop thinking about my twin brother," he said. Delani paused for a second and said, "You think they'll allow me to go to his funeral, Nurse Brown?"

The question seemed to bother her, as if she was anticipating him asking such a critical question. "I doubt it," she said softly. "But I've seen strange things happen here."

"They won't," he said simply.

"Be strong Delani."

"I need your help wit' something."

Nurse Brown didn't reply.

With one glance over at the prison guard, seeing that he was watching what was going on out in the hallway. Delani turned his gaze back on her and said. "What if I told you that I can help pay the rest of your way through college? All I need is one thang, and I only trust you to do it for me.

"How you know I need help paying my tuition?"

"The streets talk," he said.

"And now what makes you think the streets won't talk if I help you?" She said, leaning in closer to him.

Delani didn't even hesitate. "Because you're smart enough to keep your mouth shut and keep people out of your game room. Plus, you really want that degree and wouldn't do nothing stupid to prevent you from getting it," he said.

"And what you're asking of me isn't stupid?"

"No," he replied. "It's a blessing, Nurse Brown."

"Delani knew he had her roped in early when she bit the bait, so what he was doing now was putting the icing on the cake.

After a long moment, she said, "What is it?"

"Write the number down," Delani began, managing to set his plan in motion. He'd decided against the wicked thoughts he had earlier, he no longer wanted to die in prison. At least now he doesn't.

After the nurse finally took her leave, Delani laid back and shut his eyes. Again nightmares of Vermani forced themselves into his mental vision, but they were only just fuel for his motivation to process a master plan.

There were no more tears, only pure hate.

And when the day came for Delani to execute his plan, it was going to shock the world.

Chapter 9

It was two days after the incident took place when Dejah learned about the losses her team took. When she learned that Vermani had been killed along with the others, she could only imagine what Delani was going through. There was no mistaking the grief and anger he was going to experience for a very long time. She knew how Delani thought, he was plotting, and whatever he was cooking up would, no doubt, make a lasting impression.

It was the day before Vermani's funeral and Delani wouldn't be attending, which was enough to cause Dejah to worry about his mental health. Of all her youngins, she knew Delani was a little past crazy in the head, though his intelligence was something not to be denied, too.

The boy was genius, always scheming.

Dejah could feel it in her heart that something beyond her wildest dreams was about to take place.

Meanwhile, she couldn't allow herself to be distracted by what was out of her control. Dejah was facing the rest of her life in prison, if she didn't figure out a way to duck the time they were threatening to give her. Not saying she would become a rat to save herself, because snitching was totally against everything she stood for. But in due time, it would work itself out. All she had to do was be patient.

That war with Lyonell is what set the wheels spinning with the Feds. When dozens of bodies were falling around the city at one time, that was the factor that did it. Then Ced, who had been an FBI special agent, was murdered and that intensified things more.

The Feds were sneaky as hell. They watched and waited to see who would emerge from the war victoriously first, then they went in for the attack. Just when the team had accomplished their mission and was about to get back to what they were doing before, the Feds swarmed in from every angle and all directions, dismantling the whole team. Dejah was labeled the ringleader, the head honcho who called all the shots, which she was, but sill, she wasn't convinced their fall from grace was caused by the war. There was something else that happened behind the scenes, prior to Lyonell's return to get back at them.

There was a snake inside her empire, and Dejah was already in the process of locating the serpent.

Yeah. Somebody had fucked up somewhere, and thought it would do them some good to share family secrets, because on more than one occasion, when Dejah was questioned by the FBI officials, some things were mentioned that only could have come from somebody within the family. She was so raw at reverse-psychology that when the investigators thought they were using it on her, she was manipulating their minds to believe something that was so frivolous they ended up sharing what they knew. When the information was shared, Dejah went back to the room to wrack her brain thinking of who the perpetrator could be.

The shit even made her shed a few tears. She had known without a shadow of doubt that her crew was solid. But come to find out, it had been a mess the whole time.

Somebody had crossed the line. The trust was gone.

But one thing she knew for sure, neither one of the original hooliganz crew members was at fault, not Heaven, nor Jamir, Vermani, Delani, nor Shamar, and Dejah was willing to bet his life on that. She wished she was present amongst their crew to observe their response, when she called the perpetrator out, and chopped their head off. Dejah didn't tell the others of her revelation that there was a person of dishonor and disloyalty within their family. She wanted to find him on her own, then they would know, and death would be the only answer.

She wasn't alone there in the female federal holding facility. There was young Mookie and Shoo Baby with her, two of the few females who were actual members of the HCG crew. They were late recruits, after Rikah was hand-picked by Shamar himself, but both were around long enough to prove their worth. When they entered the building, Dejah and her two crew members were embraced immediately and shown the proper hospitality by the other women, who held respected positions.

Despite her foul mood and being locked up, Dejah was treated like the queen that she was.

Unlike the situation between Sonic and the hooliganz, Dejah took what was offered to her and her girls, and did whatever was allowed to make the best out of their situations.

Before long, she had used her influence and finesse game to talk a prison guard she knew and kitchen staff worker to bring in a phone and some dope and cigarettes, so her and her girls could maintain their hustle and live well. Dejah wasn't new to doing time, she'd already served a fifteen year bid, once before, so surviving behind the wall came naturally. But this time she had power and influence, two major important factors that would get her what she desired.

There were those at came around only because they expected to get something out of the deal, but Shoo Baby saw to that instantly, having to bloody her knuckle up on a few bitches to lay the law down for the others who dared to try. Both Dejah and Mookie thought it was funny how easily Shoo Baby had all the other women scared shitless.

But not everyone, to be exact, for there were others who respected the game and kept their distance. There were some stone-cold bitches in the building, killers, hustlers, and divas. It was all about respect in there.

Only the strong survived. A weak bitch didn't stand a chance, which was why she was sitting there, in her cell, at that very moment, watching as Mookie put a battery pack together to power her cell phone up. Dejah was mentally kicking herself for not spotting the snake in her crew before they sunk the whole ship. Now here she was, stuck with two of her girls, tussling with a cell phone that they had to rig up with AA batteries and wires from its prongs to the makeshift battery pack circuit, just to call home.

"Is it done?" Dejah asked, once Mookie finally sat the phone down on the bunk next to her.

"Done," she said.

Without further encouragement, Dejah picked up the cell phone and powered it up. Mookie then moved over to the cell door to keep watch for the guards and other movements. It was lock-down, the lights were off across the housing wing, which was the perfect time to get some calls in.

Dejah called Heaven for an update.

"I was hoping you called," said Heaven, the second she picked up the phone on the second ring.

"You was, huh?"

"Yeah."

"Then what's the news?" Dejah asked.

Heaven sighed, "Murder."

Chapter 10

Baby Gal had promised her mother that she would find Corey and get to the bottom of the situation.

It was after 4:00 a.m. and Baby Gal was in her Toyota Camry, parked on Bel-View Road. The traffic was light, and she could easily see the row of townhouses, especially the beige one with brown trim where she'd been told by a reliable source she'd find her brother.

The house belonged to Victoria Jones, the loyal cousin who Solo had persuaded to take Corey in. Since his falling out with their mother, Baby Gal learned that her little brother had run to Solo for help.

She should have been the first person Corey had come to, thought Baby Gal as she watched the house. Did he trust Solo more than he trusted her? What could Solo possibly do for him that she couldn't do for her own brother?

Baby Gal wouldn't have been on this mission if it wasn't for the tasks that Heaven had commanded of the team, which was to seek vengeance against those whose people had played a part in killing the hooliganz.

During that fateful mission of three days of hunting down niggas in the night and murdering them and their families, Baby Gal had received information in regards to Corey's whereabouts. But she didn't go straight to it, because after the murders, the crew fell back in the shadows and laid low. During that kill mission, Baby Gal had slaughtered individuals. Heaven was even present during one of those kills, proving that she was willing to get her own hands dirty, too.

That night, Baby Gal watched Heaven kill the mother of Sonic, slitting her throat from ear to ear, while Rikah and Gucci held her down. That very same night, Baby Gal had confided in her that Sonic's mother was her first kill.

Heaven wanted to show them all that she wouldn't mind doing what she asked them to do and that she wasn't afraid to die herself.

Baby Gal knew she was scared. She knew Heaven did what she did that night out of pride, fearful that if she didn't do it, her team would no longer respect her. It didn't take a rocket scientist to figure that out.

Baby Gal saw headlights in her rear view mirror first, but didn't realize until after they'd passed her that the car was a black Camaro 2SS.

There was an empty space in front of the townhouse, and the Camaro eased into it, parked, and shut off the lights.

It was back dark again, and Baby Gal exhaled. She looked at the watch and saw the time. It was 4:30 predawn. The typical time for a street nigga to get in after a long night out there grinding.

She watched Solo get out of the car, phone to his face and a duffel bag in the other hand. He made his way to the front door and let himself in. Lights came on in the house and Baby Gal saw Solo's silhouette against the front window curtains. Baby Gal reached for her Beretta .9mm from beneath her seat as another car came down the street, the headlights shining in her eyes. She waited for the car to pass her before getting out, but instead, it pulled parallel to the Camaro and parked.

The driver-side door opened, and to her surprise, Corey got out, carrying a leather gym bag in his grasp. Before her brother could take five steps, Baby Gal was out of her car, at once, and hurrying in his direction.

Sensing movement behind him, Corey reached for his pistol and spun around on her, aiming his banger at her as she closed the distance between them.

"Baby Gal?" He looked at her puzzled.

"What's going on? Little bro?" Baby Gal also had her Beretta in hand but non-threateningly. She stopped before Corey and he shot a nervous glance behind him at the house.

"What're you doing here, sis?"

"You've been avoiding my calls, Corey. Then you changed your number on me. What's up with that bullshit, little bro?" Baby Gal said. "I thought we could trust each other?"

"This ain't the time for this, Baby."

"Why not? You worried about Solo and what he'll say? Fuck that pussy nigga. You do know he's a rat, right? The nigga got a ticket on his head. I don't respect that nigga, nor do I agree wit' your decision to be fucking wit' him," said Baby Gal, growing angry and seeing how frustrated she was making her little brother. He was only sixteen, and from the look of it, Corey was headed down the wrong road, fucking with the likes of Solo Mitchell.

The nigga was hot as fish grease. He was in big trouble.

"I'm doing me, Baby Gal. I know mama sent you to look for me," Corey said, frowning at her.

It was at that moment that Baby Gal saw the medallion that Corey had on his Cuban link chain around his neck. She stepped forward and reached for the diamond encrusted medallion. It was the initialed pendant that stole her attention. When she saw the "BG" initials, it took everything in her not to snatch the muthafucker from his neck.

"So Bully Gang now, Corey?" She asked.

Right then, the front door of the house opened and Solo stepped outside onto the porch. He looked out at them, then he made his approach.

When Baby Gal saw him coming, she released the medallion and sneered in his direction.

"Be cool," Corey warned her.

Without even responding to her brother's warning, Baby Gal watched and waited until Solo made his way over to them. It was obvious by the look on his face that he wasn't happy to see her out there.

"What y'all got going on out here?" Solo asked. He was a tall skinny nigga, who resembled the late rapper Young Dolph, but with shoulder length dreads and big lips.

"Nothin' that concerns you, Solo," said Baby Gal.

He smirked. "If it got anything to do wit' C Murder here, then it does concern me."

"C-Murder?" Baby Gal glanced at her brother.

Corey shrugged with nonchalance.

"That's right," Solo said.

"Lil Brah don' manned up."

"You tripping, Solo." She shook her head sadly. Then she upped her Beretta and put two slugs through his head. She then stood over his body and was about to send another slug into his chest, before Corey shoved her away.

"The fuck you doing?" Corey barked at her aggressively,

"What the fuck you mean, nigga?"

Corey got up in her face. "You dead wrong for that shit, Baby. You puttin' me in a situation," he snapped.

Baby Gal saw it in his eyes and it hurt her deeply. Her own flesh and blood had chosen the enemy over her.

"You love him more than you love me, little bro? Is that what you tellin' me?" She asked.

"Just get the fuck away from me," he growled.

A silent tear fell from her eyes. Baby Gal knew that she had lost her little bro forever. She turned around and ran back to her car. When she was pulling away from the scene in her car, shots rang out in the night behind her. When she looked back and saw her little brother shooting at her retreating car, Baby Gal didn't know what to think.

Was he really trying to kill her? Or was Corey bustin' his gun just to make it look good in the eyes of those who could be watching?

"I can't believe this little nigga." Baby Gal wept as she sped through the night with a broken heart. Her little brother was gone. Corey was dead. He was dead to her now.

Chapter 11

Hours later, Heaven was sitting next to Kiara and her husband, Harold, on the front right pew, before Vemani's casket, staring from behind her dark Prada shades. Heaven struggled to keep her ears at bay. Behind her was her mother, Monica, Anya, and her four-year-old son, Malik, and her beloved second-mother LaShonda, who was in the process of gazing blankly ahead. The Greater Tanner Chapel Baptist Church was packed down with mourners. Vermani had been loved and cared for by many, and today it showed through the number of people that came to witness his last journey.

Beyond the church, at other worshiping homes, were the funeral ceremonies of the other dead hooliganz. It was a very sad day for Heaven and her people. What she really wanted was for her hooliganz to all have their final journey together. But there was no church big enough in the old small town to carry all nine caskets and their mourners all together, so that everyone would mourn together and grow in unity and harmony. Even with the moment to do it, the families of the dead hooliganz wanted to have just that one ordinary ceremony to send their loved ones off as any other should.

Heaven had no choice but to respect that, complicated but fair. She just didn't want to have to choose between whose funeral she should attend first. She loved all her hooliganz equally, and that was a fact they all were aware of.

There was no telling what was going through Delani's head at that moment. His identical twin brother was being laid to rest, in his absence. The federal District Attorney and the mayor himself denied Delani's furlough to attend his brother's funeral, stating that he was a flight risk, and while under Federal indictment, it warranted that he remained on lock down. By now, Delani was probably at his darkest stage. He was outraged. Devastated.

Heaven would give anything to have all her brothers there to join Vermani one last time. When she couldn't stand the pain much longer, Heaven kissed Kiara's cheek and rose up to her feet. She was dressed in an all-black silk pants suit and blouse, with matching pumps. With a brief nod in the direction of her mother, Heaven made her way towards the exit of the church.

In passing, numerous pairs of eyes watched her retreat, many out of sorrow and understanding, some out of contempt, because they did not agree with her dramatic change of aspiration in life. A lot of people blamed Heaven, without knowing the actual circumstances in which she was free and the others weren't. They felt that she somehow was responsible for what happened to Vermani. It was crazy how people assumed things that were not true to justify why they should feel the way they do.

As she made her exit, several of her Royal Mafia crew members got up and fell in step before her and behind her. Heaven walked out with her head held high.

It was who she saw once she stepped outside those church doors that instantly left her astonished.

"Ty?" She paused.

Then White Boy Ty, who had been sitting down on the entrance steps, glanced up at her with cold blue eyes of grief.

"TY!" Heaven rushed to his side and he stood up, only to be taken into her arms.

"I had to come back," he replied.

"But what're you doing out here alone? Why didn't you come in for the service, Ty?"

He shook his head wearily. "I can't see my brotha like that, Hev," said White Boy Ty, obviously having lost at least fifteen pounds since the fall.

Heaven hugged him again.

"I understand. I can't do it either, ya know?" Then it registered just how severe the situation was at that moment. Heaven took hold of White Boy Ty's arm and led him to her waiting SUV. Once they were settled into the back next to one another, Heaven turned back to the man to observe him more closely.

"I know, sis," Ty said in an exasperated breath. "I know I look like shit right now. Life on the run isn't all that peaches and cream either," he expressed.

"You look beautiful, Ty," Heaven said sadly.

White Boy Ty looked taken aback by her statement, although he knew she was only trying to make him feel better about himself. Heaven reached for his hand and squeezed it reassuringly.

"Where to, Hev?" said Pumpkin, from behind the wheel.

"Anywhere but here," she replied. "Just drive."

"Okay."

They were on the move. Another car pulled out behind them, loaded with armed Royals. For a long moment, Heaven just sat there, holding White Boy Ty's hand, while gazing out her side window.

"So where have you been?" Heaven asked him, turning fully around in her seat to face him.

"Key West." There was regret in his voice. "Then I read about Vermani on Facebook, and here I am."

"How was Key West?"

"Complicated," he replied.

"How so?"

He told her about spending the initial two days in hiding, sleeping in abandoned cars and breaking into houses to feed himself. Then about his hard travels south, stealing one car after another, killing a nigga down in Orlando over pocket money, and then finding rest in Tampa for a week. After which he had to kill another nigga, who called himself trying to jack him for his Jordans.

Heaven thought, *trying to jack him for Jordans,* as she looked down at his feet and saw that he wasn't wearing Air Jordans. The Nikes he was wearing now looked beat up and worn.

He went on to tell how he met a seventeen year old runaway in North Tampa who paid him twenty dollars to drive her to Miami. Once in Miami, he spent nearly a week there, too, but only after cracking the head of a petty hustler and taking everything he had. He was with Shamoorah, the runaway, who had been the one to lure the hustler in to get robbed. She had gone to Miami to meet a man that she met online, only to realize that she had been duped the whole time. So Shamoorah was kinda stuck with him, and then realized just how street crafty she was.

"Did you fuck her, Ty?" asked Heaven.

"What kinda question is that?" He blacked.

"Yeah," said Pumpkin. "He fucked her." She was grinning the whole time.

White Boy Ty said. "I fucked her, yeah. Happy now?" Then he went on to say how robbing the petty hustler led to one of his homies witnessing the whole lick.

"Shit got hectic after that and we had to get missing. Before we knew it, we had landed in Key West. That's when that little bitch spiked my drink and robbed me for everything I had. I woke up madder than a muthafucker. But I charged it to the game, and got it out the mud."

"The little runaway bitch robbed you?"

He nodded. "Yep."

Heaven chuckled at that.

"What's so damn funny?" He frowned.

"I love you, Ty. It's good to have you back home wit' us. And you got a lot of work ahead of you, too," Heaven said, laying her head against his shoulder.

"I'm beginning to see that."
"A lot has changed, Ty."
He nodded. He was beginning to see that, too.

Chapter 12

At the Juvenile Detention Center, it was the lunch hour and Jamir's housing pod was filing into the cafeteria building. Behind him was Hollow, Lil One, Zamon and Vontay, all of which were members of the HCG crew. There were several others, but their housing pod hadn't come out yet, to eat lunch.

Once they got their food trays, Jamir led the way to the four-seat iron table. Zamon sat at the table behind the rest of them, eyeing the other delinquents suspiciously, as they reluctantly sat down at his table. Today they were having pizza and French fries, which was Zamon's favorite, considering he didn't have the luxury of really eating like he wanted to.

"Lemme get that, Harry Potter." Zamon reached over and took the slice of pizza off the tray of a scrawny little white kid named Alex, who indeed had the Harry Potter look going on, with the geek glasses and shit.

Harry Potter didn't even say one word. Instead, he ducked his head and began eating what was left of his food. One knew better than to test Zamon's gangsta, and it had nothing to do with who he was affiliated with. He was a mass of destruction, all by his lonesome. That's why Jamir recruited him. Zamon was a beast.

"I got a plan," said Jamir, who was not really hungry but was taking a bite out of his pizza anyway.

"I was wonderin' when you was gonna say that," Vontay replied. He was sixteen years old and as ruthless as a pack of wolves."

"I'm listening," Lil One said.

Across the room, the middle-aged, white security guard was leaning back against the wall near the exit door. Arms folded across his broad chest, the guard checked the time on his watch and yawned into his hand.

"Y'all know the only reason we're even here, in the Tent, is because we're juveniles. We're not the same status as the others because they considered adults. I'm tired of this kiddy land bullshit," said Jamir.

"You ain't lying," said Hollow. "Just being around all these punk ass jits is depressing as fuck."

"I know a way we can change that," added Jamir.

"How?"

"We'll have to fuck some shit up," said Jamir.

"I don't give a fuck," said Lil One, a little too loudly. He attracted the attention of others.

Zamon looked back and said, "Me neither. Whatever the hell you are all talking about."

Jamir explained to his crew that in order to get away from the Tent, they would have to do something so serious that the judicial system would have no choice but to adjudicate them. That way, they would be filed as adults and no longer fit the status of juveniles. Once that happened, they would be transferred to where LJ and the other older hooligans were. At least that's what Jamir hoped, but nothing beat a failure but a try.

"What about Mr. Keats?" Whispered Vontay, when Jamir was finished with his scenario.

"Not until we alert the others on what sign is first. And we can't fuck up Mr. Keats, brah," said Jamir. "That cracka fucks wit' the hooliganz, for real."

"Yeah," Hollow agreed. "He is pretty cool," he added.

"And what about Duke, Bred Man, Taquan and Mane? They thirteen and fourteen," said Vontay.

"They too young to be tried as adults. These crackas only gonna hold them till they turn sixteen or older, before they decide to do anything wit' them."

"You right, bruh. But we're tryna get in a position where we can do more for the ones left back here. I know it doesn't sound fair to them, if we leave, but the only way we gon' make something happen is if we made that move. I want to, my nigga," said Zamon.

"You know I'm down for whateva," said Lil One.

"Then it's settled," said Hollow. Later on, back in his room that he shared with Lil One, Jamir sat down and penned a letter to Bush Boy. He was another hooligan, also sixteen and one of the most vicious ones. In the pod with him, across the easy path, was Peanut, AV, Kaden, Lil Eddie, and Sonny. Once they got ahold of the message he was writing, Jamir knew that they would be more than eager to put on. They were a loyal bunch, young and true.

"Kahlil and 'nem need us there wit 'em anyway." Lil One broke the silence between them. He had been laying on his back in the bunk, staring up at the ceiling. Jamir knew exactly what he was referring to. The loss of their brothers during the prison war with some Crip nigga named Sonic.

"We gon' get there," Jamir assured him.

Today was the funeral of their fallen hooliganz, and the pain in their hearts was raw, especially for AV and Sonny, whom Vermani had taken a liking to and recruited. Jeremy had brought Lil One to the crew, and had been proud of his decision. Lil One had cried a thousand tears the day he found out.

"Jay?"

"Yeah, brah."

"Can't you put that down for a minute? I need to tell you something," said Lil One.

"I need to get this done before the next rec. Is it more important than what I'm doing right now to execute the plan to get us the hell away from here?"

Lil One sat up on his bunk and said, "Kahlil."

"What about Kahlil?"

"I think somethin's not right wit him."

"What do you mean by something not right, Lil One? Be more direct wit' watchu saying."

Rising all the way up from his elbow and tossing his legs over the side of the bunk, Lil One said, "I didn't wanna bring it up because I know how dangerous this shit is. But I think Kahlil sold us out to them people, bruh. I know he had somethin' to do wit' that shit." Jamir set aside his writing materials.

"You need to really think about watchu saying about our big brah, Lil One," he warned. "Accusations like that could get a muthafucker killed."

"My point exactly.

"Then why the fuck would you say it, then?"

"The same reason why Kahlil was getting outta the back of a police car one night, downtown, and was handed back his gun by one of the cops, too."

"What?" Jamir bellowed.

Lil One nodded his head in response.

"When was this?"

"About five months ago, bruh."

Jamir shook his head in response.

"And are you positive it was Kahlil you saw?"

"That's on Vee," he said.

Jamir knew he meant Vermani, and that was all the clarification he needed to know that Lil One was speaking the truth.

"This is bad," whispered Jamir.

"I didn't wanna say nothing," said Lil One. "And even if he didn't rat, how the fuck can he explain what I saw that night, wit' my own eyes?"

"You know it'll be your word against his, right?"

"I know."

Jamir looked at his hooligan and saw that he was having trouble meeting his eyes now. He'd learned a long time ago that if someone avoided eye contact with you, they were either lying about something or ashamed.

"Who else was wit' you that right, Lil One?" asked Jamir, figuring that was what it was that had his friend and brother looking so damn perturbed.

No answer.

"Who was it?" Jamir insisted.

After a moment, Lil One exhaled and looked up at his hooligan's eyes. "I was wit' Booty Boo."

"The prostitute?"

Lil One nodded.

"No wonder you didn't wanna say shit," said Jamir, now faced with a whole other predicament. "Damn."

Chapter 13

The second LaShonda stepped out of the bathroom, she heard the unmistakable sound of a closed fist striking flesh. Then came the sound of a struggle being made between two people in battle. When LaShonda stopped across the hall and peered into the master bedroom. She gasped in surprise and rushed inside at once.

Kiara and her cousin, Angie, the detective, were going at it. One was fighting out of pain and hatred, while the other fought out of survival.

Kiara was trying to knock Angie's head off with the gravy blows she was throwing her way.

"Stop it. Y'all cut this shit out," LaShonda shouted as she moved in to separate the two.

Kiara had Angie by the top of her shirt, twisted into a firm grip, and was delivering some vicious punches to her face and neck area. Angie was struggling to get away.

"Harold! Tony! Somebody get in here!" LaShonda knew Kiara was in a very dark place right now, and what better way to release that rage than the very person who played a general part in creating the emotion? Kiara felt her cousin was responsible, and now one of her sons was dead? There was no denying the wrath she was experiencing. Moments later, Harold's god brothers, Preach and Anya, showed up and stepped in to intervene.

"Get Angie. Get Angie," LaShonda said. She had both of her arms wrapped around Kiara and was losing her hold.

"That's enough, Kay. Let her loose. C'mon now, we don't need this shit right now," said Preach, who was trying to pry Kiara's fingers away so Angie could get free. Anya was holding onto Angie, just for that purpose, to pull her away the instant her grip was broken.

There was no quitting in Kiara. And then Harold came in, and together, he and Preach managed to separate the women.

"Get here outta here!" Harold's voice boomed with authority. By all means, he was the man of the house. He had his wife in a bear hug, and even with his size and stretch, it wasn't no easy feat.

"Calm your ass down, woman!"

"Lemme go. I'ma kill that heifer," screamed Kiara, almost at the top of her lungs.

When Anya and LaShonda managed to get the bloody and bruised Angie out, Preach shook his head warily and left the room behind them. He knew Harold had his end under control and gave them their peace.

"Lemme go, Harold," demanded Kiara.

"You gonna behave yourself and talk to me?"

"Yeah," she said.

Reluctantly, Harold let his wife go. Kira flexed her hands a few times and took a deep breath. Then Kiara shoved her husband aside and ran for the door.

"Oh shit," Harold said, and went into a panic.

When Kiara went in search of her cousin, she found her in the kitchen, wiping blood from her face with a wet paper towel. At the sight of Kiara and the gun, everybody steered clear, staying out the way. Without mercy, she lifted the gun and bashed Angie across the face with it, dropping her to the floor.

"No Kay," somebody yelled in alarm. Kiara straddled her cousin, and was about to create the ultimate sin by killing her. But she was prevented from doing so due to the next voice of authority that penetrated her senses.

"Kiara Susan Bradwell, if you so much as put your finger on that dang trigger, I will take the gun away from you and shoot you next," the voice said. Kiara paused and looked in the direction of the voice that seemed to have stopped the world from turning.

"Now that I got your attention, put away that dang thang before you hurt someone else," said Brenda Galloway, her great-aunt and the stronghold of their family. She was standing in the kitchen doorway looking in, as multiple others looked on.

Without having to be told do so, Preach took the gun away from her and handed it over to Harold. Then another male relative helped Kiara up off of Angie, whose eyes were wide with fear of almost dying.

"Y'all should be ashamed of yourselves," said Aunt Brenda.

"It's Vermani's blessed day and y'all up in here carrying on like some dang animals."

"It's her fault." Kiara pointed at Angie.

"I don't wanna hear it," snapped the elderly woman.

Monica was easing her way through the bunch to get inside the kitchen to stand between the two cousins.

"Whateva the matter is you and your cousin need to work that out a different way than tryna kill one anotha," she said. "I taught y'all better than that."

Kiara shot a dark look over at Angie. If looks could kill...

When everything was all said and done, Brenda made the two cousins apologize to everybody for their actions. Then the repast resumed naturally, but with a little tension in the air.

Later, while Kiara was laying across Vermani's bed in his old bedroom, there was a knock at the door, but she didn't answer it. The door opened up anyway, and Heaven walked into the room.

"Thought you might need some real peace of mind," said Heaven, as she slipped off her flats and slipped into bed with the mother of her brothers. In her hands was a bottle of Hennessy, two cups, and a can of Coca-Cola.

"What do you think you're doing, Hev?" Kiara replied lazily.

"Easing my mother's wounded heart."

"That won't do it."

"It's a start," said Heaven, after pouring a cup of Hen-dog with chaser for the both of them. Then she pulled out a fat blunt of Runtz weed, and continued, "And this is what's going to end all of your worries for now."

"What makes you so sure of that?"

"Just trust me."

And trust her she did. Minutes later, Kiara was so high she didn't even know how she got there. She hadn't smoked weed in years. But her drink made it all better, as her and Heaven talked and reminisced about Vermani,

Then Heaven's phone rang and she retrieved it, looked at the caller ID and handed it over to Kiara.

"It's for you," she said. "Right on time."

"Who is it?"

"Your heart," said Heaven.

Staring down at the phone in her hand, Kiara accepted the call and put it to her ear. "Hello?"

"I love you, mama," came Delani's voice.

Her breath caught and Kiara felt her heart quicken with sudden excitement. "Denali," she cried.

Heaven kissed her on the cheek and took her leave. Her mission was accomplished.

For the next twenty minutes, Kiara and Delani talked, cried and laughed together, and it was enough for her to know that shit was graveyard serious.

"I got a plan, mama," he said.

"I know you do, baby. You always have a plan." Kiara was sure his plan was in regards to something dangerous, but worth the opportunity. He didn't have to tell her that his plan involved getting out of prison, because she knew how her son thought and what he was capable of.

"Just as long as you come back home to me, I don't care.

"I will," he told her.

"You promise?"

"I promise," he replied. "That's on my twin."

Chapter 14

When Baby gal exited the trap house on Davis Street, in the High Bridge area, she was carrying a backpack, slung across her shoulder. She got into the waiting BMW parked at the curb, and drove away.

"Now?" Said Souljah from the back seat of the dark blue Chevy Caprice Classic parked up the street.

In the front passenger seat, sat Corey, as C-Murder, with a Mac-11 machine gun lying across his lap. The cold look on his face was evidence of where his thoughts were at that moment. Since Solo's death a week ago, all he'd been doing was securing his position in the crew and contemplating his next move.

The Bully Gang was in an outrage. The pressure was up.

The night Solo was murdered was one of the hardest things he had to go through in life. Between Victoria's suspicious responses and the gang's hunger for blood, Cory had to really put up a front to convince them of his loyalty. The bitterness he now felt towards his sister and the pain from Solo's death was what kept him focused.

Somebody had to die.

For days on end, Corey had been watching Baby Gal and learning everything about what she'd been up to lately. He hadn't known she had committed herself to the new street team that was making a lot of noise in the streets. And from the looks of it, his big sister appeared to be some big shot bitch in her crew.

Well, shit was about to get even bigger, and deadly, too.

"Go," ordered Corey.

The rear doors to the Chevy opened and both Souljah and Broozy jumped out with their tools. Corey got out next, and led the kill team to their destination. It was just past nightfall and the darkness was perfect for savagery and murder.

As they charged forward, Broozy, who was built like a human tank, pushed ahead and rammed his shoulder into the front door of the trap house. The door exploded inwardly and Souljah entered the room a step behind him.

Blocka. Blocka.

Two shots to the chest of the first bitch that moved wrong, and Souljah claimed it. Still clutching his Ruger tightly in his grasp, Souljah watched as Corey chased the second bitch, who dashed from the kitchen down the nearby hallway.

"Catch that hoe, bruh," shouted Broozy.

And caught her, he did, but not before putting a bullet thought back of her left thigh. The female hustler screamed and hit the floor. Then she materialized with a gun and sent three shots at Corey, one of them grazing him across the right side of his cheek.

Boc. Boc. Boc.

Corey drilled holes into her splattering her brains all over the floor and his shoes.

"Fuck," he cursed, feeling the stinging sensation in his face and staring down at the dead woman before him. He hadn't even known she was in possession of a gun.

Broozy came up behind him and Corey told him and Souljah to check the house for the product. He knew Baby Gal had just collected from the trap house and supplied them with more product. His crew did as they were told, and eventually, the stash was located in the kitchen.

They collected and the got ghost. Mission completed.

Once back in the car, the Bully Ganga crew got the hell out of dodge. The payout was two bodies, half brick of coke, a quarter brick of heroin, some weed and two more guns to add to their collection.

Halfway back to the hood, out in the Dog Town community, Corey pulled out his cellphone to make a call. While holding a torn piece of his shirt to his face to stop the blood flow of the wound, Corey dwelled on the fact that he should have had the trap house burned down, too.

"Yo?" Baby Gal answered the phone on the fifth ring, instead of ignoring the blocked number, like she normally would.

"That's just the beginning," said Corey. "I'll see you when I see you."

"Corey?" she replied.

He disconnected the call.

At the house, Corey had Broozy's sister, Tiwanna, see to the wound on his face. The graze was deep, and hurt like hell, too. But Corey bit through the pain and decided to use it as sustenance to fuel his vengeance. He wasn't finished, by a long shot. Corey couldn't wait to disrupt his sister's motion again. Since she could not respect his mind before, she damn sure would do so now. And if that wasn't enough, he knew what would be.

He knew where to hit her and she would feel it, just like he did when she killed Solo the other night.

"You might need to get some stitches," said Broozy, entering the bathroom where Tiwanna was cleaning Corey's wound.

"What happened?" She asked her brother.

"He didn't tell you?"

"No."

Broozy chucked. "Then you don't need to know."

Tiwanna slapped Corey playfully across the head and told him to get out of the bathroom.

He rose up from the toilet lid and delivered a humbled thanks to Tiwanna. She rolled her eyes and he stepped out of the bathroom, past Broozy.

This was Corey's right hand man, Broozy, the very same one who convinced Solo to take Corey into the fold. When that happened, Solo and Corey became almost inseparable, being that they were from the same neighborhood and all. There was still time for Broozy and the other bullies. It was just that Solo had taken a great liking to him, had even so much as given him his own place to stay, which was still at Victoria's house every now and then, now that he was seeing more street action.

"Your cut on the dresser," said Broozy, after beckoning Corey over into his room, up the hall.

"Where Souljah went?" Corey approached the dresser where his cut from the lick had been divvied up. Their cuts were secured in a McDonald's take out bag.

"He left for a minute," said Broozy.

No reply from Corey.

"Wanna smoke some of that weed we got?" Broozy obviously had rolled up a few backwoods of the weed and sparked one of them up.

"Hey, Corey," replied another voice from the doorway.

Corey turned to see Da'Jhana standing in the hall, outside the room. This was Broozy's seventeen year old sister, pretty as a kiss and curious as a scientist. She liked Corey, and he kept his attraction to her neutral.

"What's up, Daj," he replied, cool as a fan.

Broozy stepped over and shut the door in her face because he knew her intentions.

"Buggin' ass," he said.

"Now, C-Murder. It's facts time, my nigga."

"What's up?"

"You mind tellin' me why in the fuck was yo' sista leavin' that house before we hit that muthafucker?" Broozy spoke from behind a cloud of weed smoke, but Corey could see clearly the dark suspicion in his eyes.

Should I lie or tell the truth? Corey thought, as he stared at his homie.

"And don't try to lie neither, nigga. You did that already. We supposed to be brothaz. No secrets amongst the brotha hood, my nigga," Broozy quoted one of their major laws and that left Corey forced to tell him the truth.

"Me and my sista are beefin' right now."

"Why?"

Corey swallowed. "Because," he said. "She crossed me."

"Crossed you how, nigga."

"By killin' Solo," Corey admitted.

The look Broozy gave him after that was priceless. It appeared somebody else might be dying tonight as well.

Chapter 15

Word about what the Royal Mafia crew did to Sonics people spread throughout the streets of neighboring counties, like a tsunami on the Coast of Hawaii. It didn't do shit but add to the buzz that Royal Mafia was already demanding out there in them trenches. If you didn't know, now you knew who was running things. By now, they had four trap spots. One was in Pepper Hill, one in Shaw Quarters, one in High Bridge, and one even up on the block at Dejah's old spot, which she had taken from Killa Don, years ago. The traps were starting to see some good money, which added to the buzz.

White Boy Ty was now seeing this with his own eyes. Heaven commanded her team so naturally, but it was no surprise to him. He always knew she had it in her to be a leader someday.

Royal Mafia was doing great. They were flourishing.

But he was back now, and that Hooliganz Crime Gang mentality was still in high demand. White Boy Ty thought it would be good to reawaken that HCG spirit. Regardless of the fact that Heaven was doing her own things, she was still HCG, and he would reclassify that position by reestablishing its power.

White Boy Ty was an honorable man, and he had mad love for Heaven. Loyalty to him was respectable, but he was Hooliganz Crime Gang through and through. There was no place for him in her new organization, so he could just rebuild HCG from scratch.

Now that he'd gone and retrieved his hidden money stash, he could afford to breathe easily. He had been dreaming about coming back home to get the stash he'd put away for a rainy day. Luckily for him, it was still there, stored away inside his Uncle Bart's house, out in Scott Town, right beneath the deep freezer, in the floor. A brick and a half of coke, fifty grand in cash, and some expensive jewelry. White boy Ty was damn near in tears when he recovered the money stash.

Then he went out and recruited five prospective crew members to join his HCG organization. Three of them he knew, without a shadow of doubt, would stand firm and hold it down thoroughly. The remaining two, they both had potential, but Ty would see to it that they got with the program, or were found floating in a river somewhere.

Within a week's time White Boy Ty had trap spots jumping in East Quincy and Havana, a piece of cake. Now all he had to do was stay focused and evolve. HCG was back in the game.

But it didn't take long for Heaven to make that call and summon his presence. The queen was intrigued by him.

"How I know you was gonna pull this move, Ty?" Asked Heaven, with a mischievous grin. She had requested that they meet up at Horizons Bookstore & Lounge, where a spoken word open-mic event was in progress.

Ty, who was on chill behind a pair of Tom Ford Dimitry Retro sunglasses, looked across the table at her and grinned right back.

"It's only right that I do," said White Boy Ty. "HCG is what raised me, sis."

"I know." She knew all too well.

He nodded, "But I'ma play the shadows, though, Hev."

"And I will support you in whatever you choose to do," she told him.

They had chosen one of the few dark corner sections of the lounge, where he couldn't be easily detected from a distance. One would have to be in their proximity to get what they wanted.

Plus, the place was heavily guarded by Royals, and they only did one thing: kill. So if a motherfucker had it in their mind to try some slick shit, they would never make it out of there alive.

"Just try not to make the wrong moves, Ty," Heaven said.

"I'm accused, sis." Ty was pleased that she accepted his decision to bring the Hooligan Crime Gang back.

Then her phone rang. It was Lacey.

"Talk to me, my love?" Heaven answered the phone and suddenly her face transformed into a look of alarm.

"Are you sure they both are dead, Lacey?"

At hearing those words, White Boy Ty removed his sunglasses and checked to see if his gun was still tucked at his waist. Heaven then bolted to her feet, and he followed suit, seeing in her eyes that some shit was about to go down.

"What is it?" He asked.

When Heaven raised her hand and snapped her fingers, Royals appeared by the dozen and escorted her to the door, with Rikah taking up the lead.

To Ty, it was amazing to see how trained the Royals were under Heaven's command. But there was no time for marveling over her power, he followed her and her team outside, and to the waiting Rolls Royce Wraith.

"What's going on, Hev?" he demanded of her, stepping before the passenger door of her car and opening it for her, receiving a stern look from Baiyina

"Get in, Ty." Heaven ducked into her car and scooted over for him to slide in beside her.

Before doing as he was told, White Boy Ty gave the signal to his unfailing hooligans, Marco and Kweli, and they broke through the crowd outside the building, headed for their car.

"Okay," said Ty, once he was inside the car with Heaven. "I need to know what's up, sis."

"Two of my girls were killed tonight," she said. Then she told him about MiMi and Tasha operating out of the trap house she had over in High Bridge. And Lacey, who had gone out to grab something to eat for the workers, returned only to find two dead bodies and her product gone.

"So, it was a robbery," said Ty.

"I don't care what it was," said Heaven. "My girls are dead and now somebody is about to die."

"And where are we going now? To the scene of the crime, Hev?" When she didn't answer, White Boy Ty said. "You need to get your fuckin' head on straight, sis. Fuck the trap house right now, assemble your team and hold that conference. Me and my hooliganz will go out there and see what we can find out for you."

"I can't ask you to do that, Ty."

"I know," he said. "I'm tellin' you what I'm about to do. You just need to get your shit done."

After a long second, Heaven sighed and said, "A'ight, God. Do you, Ty. Keep me posted."

Without a word, he leaned over and kissed her on the cheek. Then he told her driver to pull over and let him out. When the car pulled over, moments later, Ty got out and jumped into the backseat of the Dodge Magnum that Marco was pushing with no license.

"Where we headed, Ty?" Asked Kweli.

"To High Bridge," he said.

Where they came from to the reach their destination took a matter of ten minutes. Upon reaching Davis Street, it was to no surprise that the police and the whole CSI unit didn't have the area cordoned off. It appeared as if nothing had gone down there, which made the whole situation a little creepier, in a sense, like a Haunted House.

There were real dead people inside. And Lacey didn't bother to stick around after what she said she found inside.

Driving past the house in question, Marco parked at the end of street and they waited a spell. Observation was critical at that point.

"So, how are we gonna play this?" Marco asked. He already had his Glock .19 sitting in his lap and was ready to bust some heads if need be.

Right then, White Boy Ty spotted a crackhead he knew by the name of RockStar Jackie approaching the trap house from up the street. A thought came to mind of how he could use the crackhead to do his job for him.

"Bring that dude right there to me." He said.

"Say no more," said Kweli, getting out of the car and hurrying up the street to meet RockStar Jackie. In the backseat, White Boy Ty watched as other crackheads appeared out of nowhere. Then Marco was out of the car at once, moving in the opposite direction from Kweli, heading straight for his man, without being told to.

Ty waited for his moment.

It was coming.

Chapter 16

When the call came in to report the meeting location given, Baby Gal did not hesitate. She stopped everything she was doing to get there.

"What do you think it is?" asked Briana, who was one of two personal drivers that Heaven had. She and Pumpkin were the rotators and damn good drivers.

Baby Gal had a bad feeling about this meeting.

"I don't know, Bri. But we're about to see in a minute," she said, weaving her own car in traffic to reach their destination.

It was no more than thirty minutes ago when she received that suspicious call from her little brother. Corey's words of expression were heard clearly, but also puzzled her at the same time. *What was at the beginning?* She wondered. She pondered the statement Corey made. *He would see her when he saw her.* What did he mean by that? Was her little brother threatening her life? She thought about it, not sure whether she should take him seriously or not.

But she couldn't lie, her brother's phone call had concerned her, and Baby Gal now couldn't shake the feeling. Then the phone call came, asking all the Royals to report to the queen at once, making Baby Gal believe that something very troubling was in play.

Was it Corey? Was it something he did? Yeah, that phone call had her all fucked up in head. Little brother had done exactly what he knew would affect her focus. The location given was on MLK Blvd, down in the dead end, across from the community exercise track field, just up the short street from where Youngin used to live. It was from his knowledge that Heaven even knew the location existed. The HCG crew used to convene there all the time, at night. It was way off from the man highway, in the cut of a secluded area. Baby Gal pulled up at the location to see just five vehicles parked in the cut, away from the road.

"Doesn't look like the whole team here," said Brianna, getting out of the car to meet her Royals.

"What's that matter?" Baby Gal exited the car to do the same, counting only eleven Royal's out of the twenty-four that completed the whole Royal Mafia roster.

"Glad you could make it, BG," said Heaven.

"I'm here," she responded. Baby Gal looked around the group and detected some very serious faces reflecting from the moonlight overhead, in the dark sky.

"Okay, let's begin." Heaven took the floor." Tonight we lost two of our own Royals, MiMi and Tasha. They were robbed and killed over in the trap house that they were operating out of. As of now, we have so many suspects to seek vengeance on, in honor of our dead Royals. But sure enough, that time will come and when it do," she said, and looked at each one of the crew members. "I want the heads of the muthafuckaz responsible right here." She pointed at the ground in front of her. "At my goddamn feet," Heaven growled and her aggression was felt.

Silence filled the air all around them, even the crickets was scared to crick at that moment.

"Lacey? Step forward."

Lacey came to rest directly in front of her queen.

"What is your position in the trap house, Lacey?" Heaven asked without fully face her.

"Inside, guarding the product, while the server supplies the customers what they need."

Heaven nodded. "And when are you to leave your post?"

"After my twelve-hour shift is over and my relief comes," answered Lacey, evenly but nervously.

Baby Gal already knew what was about to happen before it even happened.

"And why did you leave your post, Lacey?"

"Because the girls and I wanted some Chinese food."

"You wanted Chinese food?"

Lacey nodded.

"So, while you're out gettin' Chinese food, two of our Royals are being robbed and killed, in your absence. Therefore, if you woulda been there, then Mimi woulda kept her post outside the trap, as the watcher. And maybe all three of you would be alive, and not the muthafuckers who killed them. So, I'm faultin' you for allowing this shit to even happen, Lacey," Heaved said.

"I'm sorry, Hev. It won't happen, again," Lacey pleaded.

"Somebody beat this sorry bitch to death," Heaven replied.

Immediately, three Royals pounced on Lacey, like a pack of hyenas on a bear cub.

Baby Gal watched as Lacey was being severely beating and savagely thrashed by her own crew. All she could do was try to fight back, but her attempts were to no avail, for she was no match against three Royals.

"And BG?" Heaven suddenly appeared at her side, while Lacey cried out in fear and agony behind her.

"What's up, Hev?"

"You collected from the trap house this evening, am I right?" replied Heaven.

"Yea," Baby Gal answered.

"And?"

"Lacey was not present, she had already gone. But MiMi and Tasha were both there, alive and well. I collected, supplied the re-up, and left."

"And what was the re-up?" asked Heaven.

Baby Gal told her what she already should've known. Heaven didn't like for the trap spots to be holding large amounts of product. It was too much of a risk of losing it all, due to the cops, jack boys, or just by some freak accident or another, so the trap houses were only supplied a little at a time, just to keep the flow going.

"And afterwards?"

"Straight to our treasure, Garcelle."

Garcelle was Heaven's personal accountant and secretary for the Royal Mafia organization, and someone whose honesty and morale is not to be questioned for any reason.

Heaven looked at her long and hard.

At that moment, Lacey let out a deadly cry, and was literally beaten to death. The Royals had basically stoned her to death, with literal bricks and all, creating a mess in their wake of bloodthirstiness.

"Is it done?" Heaven asked.

The Royals nodded solemnly and backed away. Lacey's bloodied and battered body was still, and dead as dead can be.

"Okay, I believe you, BG," Heaven said, addressing her again.

"You did your part. Thank you," she said.

Another brief speech was made by Heaven to her crew of Royals, warning them about not following the orders given and looking out for one another. Then she ended the meeting by assuring them that a proper investigation on the robbery-homicide was underway, headed by one of HCG's most trusted comrades.

"Ty?" One of the Royals asked.

"You better know it," said Heaven, before finally taking her leave, without a backward glance.

Another thirty minutes later, Baby Gal found herself right back parked outside, up the street from Victoria's house on Bel-View Road. There was no question what she had in her heart to do at that moment. What went down tonight had her little brother's name written all over it. Corey had been the cause of tonight's troubles.

He had gone and done something unexpected.

His statement had been clear and now confirmed.

"A'ight, Corey. You wanna play the game," muttered Baby Gal, as she got out of her car, clutching her Beretta.

"Let's play 'em then, little brother."

Then she headed straight for Victoria's front door. It was her turn, and she was playing for keeps.

Chapter 17

All it took was the promise of a hundred dollars and Rock Star Jackie, along with her smoking buddy, Dave, went out and found the person who knew something about the murders. Within the matter of forty minutes, the two crackheads brought another crackhead, whose name was Samson, back to the house where the cleaning crew was hard at work.

Since the police hadn't been called and they hadn't alerted any other unwanted or undefinable witnesses, White Boy Ty took it upon himself to clean up the mess. Together, he and his crew loaded MiMi and Tasha's bodies into a stolen van that Marco went out and jacked, and sent them off to a more secluded location, where they wouldn't be found. Both bodies were taken out of the van at the Chattahoochee River and tossed into the water, but not before their bodies were tied down with cement blocks to keep them from floating back up anytime soon.

There were probably thousands of bodies in that river already. It was one of the common drop-off spots.

"What do you know?" Ty asked Samson, skeptical that he had any valuable information to provide. It's known that a crackhead would do or say anything just to get a hit, but luckily for White Boy TY, he could discern the difference between a lie and the truth, when told by a dope addict.

They always give themselves up. Ty knew this for a fact, because both of his parents were stone cold crack fiends.

"It was the Bully Boys that did it," said Samson, a middle aged black man, who was wearing a Lakers jersey and a pair of charcoal gray chuck pants and boots. When White Boy Ty really looked at him, all he could do was shake his head.

"And how do you know this for a fact, Samson?" Ty had heard talk about a Bully Gang putting in work in the streets, but he doubted he knew any of them personally.

"I know because one of them is my nephew. Man-Man. It was one of his partnaz I saw leavin' the house t'night."

"Was Man-Man wit' them, too?"

"No."

"How many was there?"

"Only three."

"And do you know any of their names, Samson?"

Samson seemed to give off a precise expression, as if he was trying to recollect the name.

"Not the ones that I saw t'night. Like I said, my nephew rolls wif them Bully Boys and I see them all the time together."

White Boy Ty thanked Samson for his cooperation and honored his word to RockStar Jackie and Dave, by providing them the hundred dollars. She snatched the hundred dollar bill and balled it up into the palm of her head. Then, up the street she went, with both men on her heels, as they argued back and forth about where they were going now, to cop some crack, since MiMi and Tasha were dead.

"Kweli?" Said White Boy Ty, stepping down from the front porch.

"I already know, my nigga," Kweli replied.

"Do it quietly."

Kweli nodded and went after the three crack heads to take them out of their misery.

The last thing the Royal Mafia needed was two dead bodies of their own to bring unnecessary attention to them. So Ty figured it was best that he kept those deaths under lid for the time being.

By the time Heaven called for a report, White Boy Ty told her he had a name, but wouldn't speak over the phone. So, they agreed to meet up at her old spot out in Pepper Hill. When heaven saw how filthy he and his crew were, she immediately demanded that he go shower.

"Now what do you have for me?" Heaven asked, the moment he had stepped from the bathroom and dried off with a thick, purple towel.

White Boy Ty told her what was told to him.

At the mention of Bully Gang, the recent incident regarding the murder of Solo Mitchell was brought up, along with the serial killing that took place after the incident, where the Bully Gang was going around seeking answers. Although they hadn't touched one of her own, until now, Heaven wondered what led them to have the right to do what they did tonight.

The Bully Gang wasn't a large organization. They really only just started making noise during the period when Lyonell had retired with his vengeance. Their gang was run by board members, selecting who they felt was worthy to be a part of their organization. There was no ranks, no set positions, they all were equal and picked according to their beliefs and their personalities. It was a complicated construction, but they seemed to have their own shit figured out.

"Who are those so-called board members?" Toby wanted to know. She was also familiar with the new street gang that was now becoming a serious problem.

"There's four of them in all," said Heaven, with Rikah and Gucci standing on either side of her. "Reggie Pittman, Flame Harrell, Tito Sanders and No Good Reynolds."

"No Good?" White Boy Ty paused instantly and frowned. "That bitch ass nigga supposed to be dead."

"He is," said Heaven. "Remember, y'all took him out already?"

"Then why is his name included?"

"Because it's Lil No Good that I'm speaking of, Ty. His son," said Heaven. "And I'm hearing that little muthafucker is calling some big shots for his gang."

They were occupying the childhood home Heaven had grown up in. Thanks to the blessing of the universe, she now owned a mini-mansion, not too far from the Governor's Mansion and that of a new, well-known politician. But despite what was going on at that moment, Heaven relished the comforts her childhood home still provided.

White Boy Ty was totally in discomfort.

"So do we be cordial about it and go to the board members first, or just take it straight to 'em and destroy them all?"

"Did they use cordiality wit' us, Ty?" Heaven answered.

He shook his head.

"Do you think they're prolly blaming us somehow wit' what went down wit' Solo?" Asked Gucci.

"You know Solo had a fifty thousand dollar hit on his head, right?' Just nobody couldn't catch him slippin' to claim it," Redd said from the kitchen doorway. "Heard he had slumped some big time dope boys up in Atlanta."

"I also heard he's an informant, too," added Meesha.

"We're gettin the fuck off track right now," Ty spoke up, and everybody shut their mouths. "What we need to be concerned about is how we're gonna play this shit out, wit' out involving the Fed's again. Because another war, right now, will be bad for business, and we need to be smart about it. Shit is going too good for us, right now, to be going to war and making our own shit hot," he stated evenly.

"So is it peace you want, Ty?" Rikah asked.

"Bully Gang is an organization based on principles and naturally being bullies. They take what they want, they extort niggaz, but I know that they don't do murder robberies. This was done without the board member's consent," explained Heaven.

"And if it was?"

"Then they're in violation and need to be dealt wit' accordingly, on top of compensating us for our losses," said Redd. "Because we still gotta get ours in the process."

"So we act on some mob shit?" Ty replied

"Who are we, Ty?" Toby interjected.

"Royal Mafia," said the Royals in unison.

White Boy Ty could only nod his head in acknowledgement.

"Royal Mafia," Heaven said passionately. Then she pulled out her cell phone to make the call. She would be cordial about the situation because Lord knows another war would create a major problem for them.

And if the Bully Gang did not comply?

No pressure. Royal Mafia was going to get theirs one way or another.

Chapter 18

Meanwhile, Shamar was in the process of stretching his arms in his prison cell, when the guard was making her mail call rounds for the night. Mail calls usually are done earlier, just after shift change at eight o'clock, but things had been postponed due to an emergency traffic call. Somebody had nutted up in the neighboring dorm and all nearby offices were radioed in to come assist the others. That's why she was coming around so late. It goes down up in the building. Every day a muthafucker was either getting shanked or their heads burst. It was a jungle in the federal facility, and if you wasn't about that life, it was best that you not even show your face.

Also occupying a cell with Shamar, was some other dude from the Jacksonville, Florida area, who went by the name of K-Gutta. K-Gutta was several years older than Shamar, a member of the Kutthroat Gang, which originated in Duval County, but was created in honor of the New Orleans Cutthroat Committee organization. But K-Gutta was a solid nigga, who was facing a federal gun possession case after selling a semi-automatic to an undercover federal agent. Shamar was grateful for K-Gutta's knowledge of how the prison affairs were of dire concern, and his wisdom on legal cases that best fit Shamar's situation. It was because of K-Gutta that Shamar spent a lot of his time researching cases in the law library.

"Knowledge is power," K-Gutta once told him. He was facing a fifteen year bid upstate and wasn't even worried because he claimed there was an error in his case that could get him his freedom back.

As he continued to flex his sore arms, after recently being stabbed in them during the battle with Sonic and his people, Shamar heard the female guard stop outside his door and slide an envelope underneath the cell door.

"Enjoy, Shamar," she replied.

"Thank you, Mz. Wilson." Shamar read the expression on her pretty face as he nodded and proceeded make her rounds. There was something in that look that made him believe she was warning him about something.

Then he knelt down to retrieve the manila envelope off the floor, and was instantly astounded by its heftiness. Shamar opened the seal, peered down inside the envelope, and gasped in absolute surprise at what he saw.

"Yo, K-G," he called out.

"What's up?" K-Gutta was laid back his bunk, reading an urban novel called "When It Rains It Pourz" by an author named Trigger, who was from Quincy. When he looked up at Shamar, he saw a look of alarm on his face.

"Cover the window for me, bruh!"

"For what?"

"Just do it, K-G!"

K-Gutta set his novel aside and threw his legs over the side of his bunk. "What kinda shit are you on, Mar?" He asked, his foul smelling feet permeating the air.

Reaching into the medium size manila envelope and withdrawing the iPhone that was inside, K-Gutta cursed under his breath and scrambled across the room to hang his towel up over the window of the door.

Shamar made his way over to the small table and chair to sit down. He set the cellphone aside and reached back inside the envelope for the letter of instructions. The letter was written by Delani, explaining to him how he was making high pay from up in the infirmary department. He assured Shamar that he was able to get five cellphones in and the others were being delivered to LJ, Kahlil, and Bizzy. The cell phones were already activated, and programmed with the contact numbers of the other hooliganz.

"Who is it from?" K-Gutta replied.

"D-Murda," said Shamar, using Delani's street handle.

"You got it made like that, nigga? You the truth, Slim," K-Gutta was saying, as Shamar finished reading the letter and ripped the paper up into shreds, before giving it to his cellmate to flush down the toilet.

Shamar couldn't believe how Delani was even able to make moves like that in the federal facility. The place was supposed to be sealed tight from such things as smuggling phones into the institution. But Delani made it happen, and that was the beginning of his charm.

Hooliganz Crime Gang was still making moves. Fuck the Feds!

Without wasting any more time, Shamar powered the phone up and called Heaven. He knew she was going to scream when she saw it was him.

"What?" Heaven answered on the first ring, startling Shamar by the aggression in her voice.

"I know Mama Monica ain't teach you to answer the phone like that, sis," said Shamar.

A sharp intake of breath was heard over the phone. "Shamar? Is this really you?" She replied.

"It's me."

Heaven didn't scream, though.

"What's the matter, Hev?" He was concerned. Shamar knew he had to keep his voice low so as to not allow anyone to overhear him beyond the door.

Another deep breath came over the phone.

"Is this phone secured?" asked Heaven. He told her it was.

In exchange, Heaven gave him the full lowdown on what was going on in her life. She didn't sugar-coat nothing with him. Shit was hectic out there and Heaven was still standing firm against the challenges. Minutes later, an incoming call came in, alerting Shamar that it was LJ calling. When he told her who it was, Heaven suggested he merge the call, so they all could communicate.

"Bae," Heaven cried happily when she finally heard her man's voice. Shamar allowed the two lovebirds to get their moment in, and Khalil, too, who was also on the line with LJ, when the line was merged in. It was a reunion phone conference, and a very emotional one.

"Now tell me what's going on," said LJ, once he was reassured that his family was good and safe. Now he wanted to know why Heaven had that edge in her.

"It was crucial out here, y'all," she said.

"Tell me about it." She reiterated what she'd told Shamar already, going further into what had been happening lately. To hear that Heaven was leading her own empire came as a great surprise to all of them, but when she explained to them what her position entailed, they all had to respect her mind.

"And guess who else I got wit' me?"

"Who, sis?" asked Shamar.

When White Boy Ty came over the phone, Shamar and the others almost blew the roof off with excitement. But LJ had to remind them all to stay low-key. They couldn't blow their cover.

"My favorite White Boy," laughed Khalil.

"I'm black, nigga, get it right," White Boy Ty retorted.

Just hearing his voice gave the hooliganz hope, especially when he expressed that he was the head of the HCG now and was keeping the legacy alive.

"Just make sure you take care of Hev for us, bruh," LJ said with a serious tone of voice.

"Trust me, y'all, Hev is doing the damn thang. But I got the fam on my end, y'all just do your parts in there. Keep your heads up and know it's HCG for life," White Boy Ty said, and got the expected response back from his brothers.

After about an hour of aligning and reaching a mutual understanding together, the hooliganz signed off to allow LJ to have his privacy with his woman. K-Gutta was then handed over the phone, so he could get in contact with his family. In the process, Shamar went into deep thought about all he'd just learned. Although it was good to hear from Heaven, he still couldn't help but worry about her. They weren't supposed to leave her out there alone to fend for herself. Somehow, someway, they had to get out of there. But Delani claimed he had a plan that would set them free, even if it was not to be done legally. Delani always had some master plan.

He was a genius.

And all Shamar could do was wait and be patient until the universe decided his true fate.

He wasn't scared at all.

He wasn't even tipping.

He was a Hooligan, plain and simple.

Chapter 19

Corey and Broozy was in the process of sparking up their second blunt of loud and waiting on Souljah to slide back through. Souljah was supposed to ditch the car they had stolen earlier for the mission, and bring back another one. It had been way over an hour now, and he hadn't even come back or called.

"The fuck this fool at?" said Broozy. He and Corey were standing outside his waiting.

Cory didn't even bother to answer as he snuck glances back at the front windows of the house. Da'Jhana was making an effort to be seen by him, letting him know that she was checking for him.

A pair of headlights turned out on the street up ahead, and was cruising forward.

"That's prolly has ass right there," said Broozy, growing very impatient with waiting on Souljah to show up.

The car drove right on by them.

Corey passed his brother the blunt, he could ease his nerves later. In mid reach, his cell phone buzzed to life with an incoming call. He reached into the pocket of his black cargo shorts for the phone.

Victoria was calling. Since Solo's death, she'd been leaning on him for support. She was ten years his senior, independent and fine as a muthafucker, and she just recently gave him the pussy for the first time. Although he knew she was vulnerable during her grieving Solo's murder, Corey took advantage of the opportunity and gave her that young thug loving. Victoria had been constantly calling ever since, sprung off the dick. And Corey liked it, too. It assuaged his pride. He'd bagged a bad older bitch.

"What's up, Vicky?" He replied, knowing she was calling to see if he was coming home tonight.

Boc! Boc! Boc! Boc!

The three blasts on the other end of the phone sent Corey reeling back and staring at the phone in puzzlement. Then he put the phone slowly back to his ear.

"Hello? Vicky? What the hell was that?" He demanded.

"Your turn, little brotha. We can play this game all night if you want to," Came Baby Gal's voice over the phone.

Heart suddenly pounding hard in his chest, Corey knew, without a doubt, his sister had just killed Victoria. The murderous tone in her voice was just as profound as the sound of the three gunshots.

"Why are you doing this?" He asked. "Why?"

"Shoulda just left shit alone, Corey. Now you done gone and played yourself outta pocket."

"You dead wrong, sis."

"Naw, young nigga, you dead won't," she hissed, like a venomous cobra. "Your turn."

When she hung up the phone, Corey knew right then that she was no longer the sister he once knew. *How did I let this shit go this far?* He asked himself.

"Don't tell me you don' made your sista kill Vicky, too, brah?" Broozy said grudgingly.

Reluctantly, Corey nodded his head miserably. He couldn't, for the life of him, think of how in the hell he could get out of this situation.

Before either one of them could speak up again, another car with dark tinted windows pulled up outside the front of the house. The horn honked once, and Broozy slapped Corey across the shoulder and made his way towards the car.

"Bout time this fool showed up," said Broozy.

Corey followed suit, but with a heavy heart, believing he'd bit off more than he could chew with Baby Gal. A few yards away, the driver door swung open and Baby Gal jumped out of the car with her gun. She filled Broozy's chest with hot lead, and he fell to the ground, dead. Corey was stunned beyond belief, as his sister walked up to him and put her pistol to his forehead. Right then, his life flashed before his eyes.

"You thought this shit was a game, huh?" She snarled in his face, patting him down and relieving him of his own gun.

"Now Strip."

"What?' He stammered.

Baby Gal went across his face with his own gun and Corey began to panic.

"Aww."

"I said strip, nigga," she growled.

Knowing that his sister was dead serious, Corey stripped down to his boxers and socks.

"Why you doing this shit, Cassandra?" He whined.

Boc! Boc! Boc! Boc!

Corey damn near jumped out of his skin when Baby Gal lifted the pistol towards his head and let loose rounds. He even heard the zoom of every bullet fly past his right ear. But she was not trying to shoot him. She sent rounds at the house, when the front door opened up.

It wasn't open anymore.

Whoever it was that opened it in the first place surely wouldn't be doing that again.

"Consider yourself warned, Corey," said Baby Gal.

"Don't fuck wit' me," she sneered at him.

Moments later, Corey watched his sister hurry back to the car and speed away with his belongings.

"Corey," came Da'Jhana's fearful cry. When he turned around towards her voice, Corey couldn't believe what he saw next.

Tiwanna, holding her bloody middle, stumbled out of the front door, with Da'Jhana half carrying her. She had been shot and was in need of medical attention.

"Please, Corey. Help," Da'Jhana cried.

Now he was really scared.

Right then, Souljah pull up on the scene in a navy blue Hyundai Elantra. Without second guessing his proration, he ran over to Tiwanna, and with Corey's help, they got her loaded into the car and were gone.

"What the hell happened, brah?" Asked Souljah.

Corey was in shock. Da'Jhana was beside herself in panic. Tiwanna was making it hard for him to think. Plus, Corey was at a loss for words. Shit was real.

Chapter 20

It had been one helluva night. When the sun rose in the sky, the next morning, so did Aaliyah Renee, pushing the bedroom door open to peer inside to see if he mother was there. A bright smile spread across her little her face. Behind her, Monica watched as her granddaughter entered the large bedroom and proceeded to try and pull herself up onto the bed.

"NaNa…" Aliyah looked back over at her grandmother, after several failed attempts to climb the bed. Monica stepped forward and lifted the child onto the bed with her mother.

Now beaming brightly and beautifully, Aaliyah pulled the cover back from Heaven's face and placed big, wet, sloppy kisses on the cheek. Her eyes slowly opened and Heaven gazed up at her daughter lovingly. Then she wrapped her arms around her baby girl and snuggled in bed with her.

"Get up, mommy," Said Aliyah, fussing at her, but snuggling in deeper under her mother.

"I don't want to, Ali. You feel so good." Heaven nuzzled her face into Aaliyah's warm neck area. She was really tired, after getting in some time after three that morning. She had a long night of directing missions and waiting on The Bully Gang board members to do their part.

"You may as well get up, Hev. You got work to do. Plus, their waiting on you downstairs," said Monica, from the foot of the large queen size bed.

With a loud groan, Heaven shook herself and Aaliyah, and decided to finally get out of bed.

Fifteen minutes later, she was fully dressed and entering the downstairs kitchen. Adjacent to the kitchen was the spacious dining room, with a ten-seat glass table beneath a beautiful chandelier, with burgundy carpeting. Upon entering the kitchen, there, surrounding the wide island counter, was Rikah, Anya, Toby, and Redd, all of whom Heaven had welcomed to stay in the seven bedroom mansion. The Royals Estate consisted of a servants' quarters building in the back of the house, which Rikah claimed as her own living space. There was also a gym room and a small movie theater room. There was a pool house in the back, along with a large pool, and modest size greenhouse structure. Monica just loved spending a lot of her peaceful time tending to her flowers.

The Estate was, by far, the house of Heaven's dreams, and she was going to do her job of keeping it.

"Good morning, Queen," said Toby, as she bumped fists with Heaven, in greeting.

Heaven spoke to everybody, and then stepped over to kiss her baby brother, Malik atop his curly head. The four year old boy looked every bit of Marlon, when he was that age. The boy giggled as he bit into his jellied toast. He had bread crumbs all over the place.

"Any word on Bully Gang yet?" asked Heaven. She slid onto the tall chair next to Redd, at the counter. She bumped shoulders with the older female gangster, and Redd one arm hugged her across the shoulders.

"As of now, they're still investigating the situation," said Redd, with her coffee sitting before her.

Checking the time on her watch, and seeing that it was just before eight o'clock, Heaven said, "They have fifteen more hours to get it done. No exceptions. And as for MiMi and Tasha, we will just tell their families that they fell in love and decided to go live happily elsewhere. We all know Tasha was swingin' that way, and MiMi fell victim, and now they're doing their own thang."

"It's a far-fetched excuse, where MiMi's concerned, but okay," said Anya.

"Love is a powerful thang," said Redd.

"It is," muttered Heaven.

Anya then placed her plate of scrambled eggs, bacon, and toast in front of her, with a glass of apple juice, and Heaven dug in.

"What's poppin' on social media?" she wanted to know.

The top stories were of Broozy and Victoria's murders, then those three crack addicts found dead on the back porch of a neighbor's house from smoking bad dope. That was definitely White Boy Ty's work, his move to hush the incident with Mimi and Tasha. But it was the story detailing the death of Broozy and Victoria that Heaven found intriguing, and worth concerning herself over.

"That's two losses on Bully Gang's side, huh?" said Rikah with the shake of her head.

"Bully Gang?" Heaven paused.

Rikah nodded and told them how she spent numerous hours investigating Bully Gang and their members, and knew a lot of them personally.

"Victoria was Solo's first cousin, and Broozy was the son of one of Solo's closest recruiters."

"And what's the streets saying that's not on social media, Toby?"

"Are you ready for this?" asked Toby.

"Speak."

"Word on the streets is that a female was behind both murders," said Toby. "Whoever that female is, I don't know. But what I do know is there's a witness to the shootin' who happened to survive the hit."

"Who?"

"Broozy's sista," said Rikah.

Heaven didn't like the sound of that. Now she was wondering who the female was and whether Bully Gang was thinking her crew was responsible or not.

"She's over at the hospital now, in the ICU, after getting shot in the stomach," said Toby.

"I wanna know who this female killa is," said Heaven. "Redd get on top of that for me."

"It's done," said Redd.

Another hour later, Brianna was behind the wheel, swerving through traffic, with Heaven laid back in her 2017 Bentley Continental GTC GT V8, which Dejah once owned, before passing it on to the next queen. Also occupying the vehicle with them was Redd, who was engaged in a phone conversation with one of the Royals.

They were there to meet Redd's people at the Tallahassee Greyhound Bus Station. It was Andrea Motley, who was recently released from prison, after a ten year bid for violent charges. She was also vouched for by Dejah, as well. So, Heaven was anticipating the meeting with Andrea and hoped she was about that life, like she had heard.

Heaven's cell phone rang. It was Dejah.

"Good mornin', Dej," she greeted her mentor humbly.

"Clean up your mess and stick to the script, Hev," said Dejah.

"Huh?" Heaven stiffened.

Dejah said, "It's too much going on in your backyard. Clean it the fuck up. Quiet and easy. Today."

When the phone line disconnected, Heaven was left thinking she was doing something wrong. She needed to regroup. What Dejah was saying in so many words was that there was too much heat in her midst that needed to be cooled down.

"Alright, Dejah," Heaven whispered to herself. "I gotchu."

It was time to change up her game. Quiet and easy.

Chapter 21

He saw them before they saw him. Good thing Corey wasn't in the room at that moment, or else he would have found himself in a trap.

In passing, Kweli heard Souljah, who was leading the pack of Bully Gang members to Tiwanna's room, threatening to do something dirty to Corey for creating trouble for them. Souljah announced that he was in violation and was about to be dealt with accordingly. Kweli had heard all of this and was glad Corey had left the room. It had been about ten minutes since Corey had been gone, but Marco was on his trail though, keeping a close eye on young goon.

The cat was out of the bag now. The Bullies were on the move, and Corey was in trouble. White Boy Ty was also in the process of reaching out to Baby Gal, in regards to her little brother. He also felt there was something behind her not being forthcoming about Corey. His whereabouts the night before were in question, as well. A conspiracy was suspected.

When White Boy Ty returned to the hospital waiting area, after making his call, Kweli informed him of the Bully Gang's mission to find Corey and smash him.

"I saw 'em when they came through just now," said Ty.

"So, what do we do now?"

Text Marco to see where he was, that's what they did. Marco replied back that he was around back with Corey.

"Go get the car ready," Ty said.

"Say no more." Kweli hurried after White Boy Ty, who was in disguise and headed for the exit.

It didn't take Ty long to locate Marco and Corey. He found them both out back, smoking a joint. Apparently, Marco had persuaded him to trust him enough to share his. When White Boy Ty pulled up on the scene, a look of cautiousness crossed Corey's face, making him instinctively move his hand near his waist.

"Don't do that," Marco reached over and laid a hand on Corey's arms to stop him. "You don't wanna do that, playboy." They quickly drew his .45 and cocked it back to chamber a round. Seconds later, a white Lincoln Town Car drove up and came to a stop before them. Kweli was behind the wheel, and from the look on his face, it was decided he was on demon-time.

"You got two options, Corey," said White Boy Ty.

Marco pulled out his Glock .9mm next, causing Corey to look at him in alarm.

"You can either get in that car, right now, or die right here, right now. You pick. And we don't have all day," he announced.

"Plus, that nigga, Souljah, and them Bully niggaz inside right now, lookin' for you," Kweli added his two cents.

"And it don't look good," Ty replied.

"This doesn't look good," said Corey evenly.

Marco upped his banger, bashed Corey across his head with it, and took his gun. Then White Boy Ty snatched him up and shoved Corey towards the car. They got in and Marco locked it on the closed side of Corey. Now he was really looking worried.

"You know where to go, my nigga," Ty said to Kweli.

"Sho' ya right, RayRay," Kweli imitated the voice of one of the actors in the old classic movie *South Central*. Then he eased off into traffic, headed back towards town. They were headed back over to Pepper Hill for trial.

It was about to get interesting, and deadly.

Chapter 22

Once again, when the call came for her to show face, Baby Gal was making her morning rounds to make sure all the trap spots were good. Toby was to replace MiMi, Tasha, and Lacey with three more qualified girls, so Baby Gal visited the latest murder scene trap house to inspect its condition. The front door needed to be replaced and just a little more blood needed to be cleaned up. But that was no problem, the new girl would see to it that it was handled.

Now on her way to Pepper Hill, where her presence was needed. Baby Gal had a bad feeling something worth worrying about was going down.

She knew all about Heaven meeting with the Bully Gang board the night before. She was present, along with the other Royals, to escort Heaven to the meeting location. Baby Gal knew there would be some suspicion as to who the woman was that was causing all the hell between their crews. An investigation was under way and new a development must has come forth.

After the incident with Corey last night, Baby Gal felt that she had done too much. The whole situation had taken her to another state of mind, where she wasn't moving strategically. Her actions were intended to prove to her little brother that she would nut up, if he didn't get his mind right, even if it meant knocking his little ass upside the head to show him shit was real.

A premonition inflamed her consciousness.

Baby Gal didn't want to go to the location, but she knew if she didn't, shit would get very drastic for her. Heaven would send for her, and if found, the Royals would be commanded to do her dirty, a for sure homicide.

To Pepper Hill she went, but not without wondering if her time to die had finally come. The location was the old Clarey's Hotel, near the Steven School Park, in one of the rear hotels rooms, away from the main room. Upon reaching the location, Baby Gal spotted three cars she knew belonged to the Royals, but there were three vehicles parked in the vicinity that were not familiar to her.

Two Royals were posted outside the last room door, Baiyina and TapTap, who appeared to still be seething after what took place with Lacey the night before. She wasn't there to witness the violation, but it was obvious that she was angry. Lacey had been a dear friend and loyal sidekick. TapTap was looking for a reason to spazz out on a bitch. She wanted some smoke. She was hurting, and this Baby Gal was aware of, as she got out of her car and approached the door.

"Hold on, BG!" Baiyina stopped her before entering.

"Gotta pat you down and take your gun," she said.

"Take my gun?" Baby Gal looked at her in offense.

"Were just following orders, Baby Gal. Respect that," said Baiyina, short and super-thick for her stature.

One look at TapTap, and seeing the stern look on her face, Baby Gal sighed in frustration and assumed the position. In the process of patting her down, Baiyina told Baby Gal that there were other people inside, besides Royal Mafia.

At hearing this, Baby Gal allowed her weapon to be taken away from her and was granted entry. When TapTap opened the door, and Baby Gal stepped inside, she halted immediately at what she saw.

"Thank you for coming, BG," said Heaven, leaning against the far wall of the room.

"Come. Come. Come." She waved her forward, and Baby Gal found herself unable to move.

Sitting in the middle of the room, tied to a chair, was none other than her little brother, Corey. He looked like he'd been beaten severely. Standing next to his chair was a woman Baby Gal had never seen before. Her hands were bloody, her clothes were bloody, evidently the results from beating up on Corey, while he was bound to the chair.

Suddenly, Baby Gal was shoved roughly from behind, and she stumbled forward into a vicious uppercut blow from the strange woman. Next thing she knew, a gun was pressed to her head by Rikah, and another by Meesha, forcing Baby Gal to believe that her ending had come.

"So." Heaven pushed away from the wall. "It appears that all of my troubles have been created from your personal grudge against your lil brotha. Explain," said Heaven.

Spitting out globs of blood from her busted mouth, Baby Gal said, "I only wanted what was best for Corey. When I heard he was involved in some deep street shit, I later found out he was under Bully Gang's influence."

Then she went on to say how she felt about Corey siding with a hot nigga, such as Solo. Her killing Solo sparked the hate in Corey that motivated him to seek vengeance on her by robbing the trap house and killing its workers.

"All that shit is what we got outta Corey already," Heaven replied.

"My question to you is this. Why did you betray my trust by not telling me the truth, when I gave you the opportunity?" She growled.

"Because I felt I could handle the situation on my own."

"That you can handle the situation? Okay." Heaven sighed and looked down at Corey's bloody and battered face, lifting his head up with a finger to see that he was very much conscious.

"You know what happens next, right?" She looked back at Baby Gal.

"Please don't make me do this, Hev."

"You did this to yourself, BG. Now you gotta *handle* the situation. It's your duty."

"But that's my little brotha," Baby Gal said.

"And MiMi and Tasha were my sistaz, my Royals."

Baby Gal's eyes brimmed with tears as she knew there was no talking her way out of this one.

"And if you ask us to kill you instead," Redd spoke up from behind Baby Gal, "he's gonna die anyway."

"Your choice," Heaven replied, before glancing down at her watch and back at Baby Gal.

"You got two minutes."

Right then, Corey slowly lifted up his head as Baby Gal stared at his bloody and swollen face. Silent tears spilled from her eyes, shielding her brother's fearful gaze. Then the sound of Rikah thumbing back the hammer on her pistol, caused her heart to skip beat.

Could she kill her own little brother? Wondered Baby Gal, as she cried before her crew and a total stranger.

"Thirty seconds," said Toby.

Without even saying a word, Heaven drew her gun, put it to Baby Gal's head, and squeezed the trigger.

Blocka!

"Fuck all that waitin' shit, Andrea?" Heaven turned towards the unknown woman also occupying the room.

Andrea was her name. She was Redd's new recruit, the one who'd just arrived fresh off the Greyhound bus. Andrea didn't need to be told what to do. She stepped behind Corey and snaked her arm around his neck.

"No," Corey cried out, just before his neck was snapped and he was left sitting there, slumped in his chair.

"Now you are Royal Mafia," Heaven replied.

Andrea only nodded her head.

Redd smiled sweetly. She had chosen wisely.

Chapter 23

That very same morning, Jamir, Hollow, Zamon, and the rest of their crew were ready for their mission. It was going down. Today they were leaving the Tent and never camping back, especially after what they were about to do.

"As soon as they opened the doors for us to go to education," said Hollow, ready with his weapon.

Jamir nodded. "As soon as," he said.

Education was a mandatory thing for the boys and girls there at the Tent. It was court ordered that they undergo schooling, while they were there. Of course, some didn't give a fuck about their education. They attended just to get out of the housing pod.

The hooliganz were ready to attend their first period of classes for the day. When the classes were over, the guards opened up the classroom door, which led to a narrow hallway. That same hallway led to their classrooms and the civilian teachers. Once that time came, it was open season for all the hooliganz.

Some were strapped with weapons taken from the shower drains, wooden book shelves, and even jagged concrete instruments pulled up from the outside basketball court and made into knives. The hooliganz were war ready. Everybody was waiting for Jamir to lead the charge.

When that time came, the guard, who everybody called Tom Hanks, announced that it was time to go to classes. What was amazing about this mission was the fact that Jamir and his crew would also be interacting with Bush Boy and the other hooliganz in their pod. They would then pass by each other in the hallways, going to their classes, too.

"Single file line, boys," Tom Hanks announced.

"Yessir," the hooliganz said in unison, as they all got in line to move out.

There were fourteen of them in all, and five of them were hooliganz, enough to get the party started.

Standing at the door, holding it open, Lil One gave each of his brothers the look as they all filed out into the hallway. Zamon kept close to the back of the line, so he could assist Lil One, when shit popped off.

And then it popped off.

When everybody was filed out into the hallway, Lil One and Zamon rushed back inside the classroom to attack the male teacher.

But Jamir had already pulled out his weapon and rushed Tom Hanks hard, stabbing him in his face and head, which initiated the showdown. Then Hollow and Vontay ran up the hallway, into the next classroom, where a female teacher was waiting. She was a total bitch, which is why she got the business.

Around the corner, on the other side, Bush Boy and his crew were bringing the noise.

It was absolute chaos in the building.

When the Code Red alarm rang, enforcements came by the droves. The hooliganz were in for a rude awakening. No longer were they considered children. It took grown ass men to step in and man-handle them all into compliance. A few of the hooliganz were punched in their faces and slammed on the ground with no regards of their safety.

Shit had gotten real.

When the higher ups showed up, the hooliganz were taken to the main administration building. There, they each saw medical and then were shoved into a cold holding cell.

"Y'all good?" Jamir asked his crew, as they waited inside the holding cell.

"I'm amped!" Lil Eddie was up, bouncing up and down on the balls of his feet.

"I see that," Zamon smirked.

That was when Hollow got up and hugged his HCG crew members that he hadn't gotten the opportunity to embrace since they arrived at the Tent. The hooliganz had all been separated from the others, up until that point.

It was a reunion.

The brothers all gave one another some dap and a hug to show some love and respect for each other.

"We did that shit," said AV.

Kaden and Lil One had caught the brute of the incident, when the enforcement came. The male guards literally put their hands on them like they were grown men. They both were sporting black eyes and busted lips, and even a broken finger in the process.

Jamir was injured, too. Two guards had pounced on him in retaliation for what he did to Tom Hanks.

Tom Hanks was being transported to an outside hospital, due to the injuries he had endured.

Two and a half hours later, the local Sheriff's department deputies showed up with some TPD officers to ship the hooliganz over to the Leon County Jail. They were all cuffed, shackled, and loaded into transport vehicles that took them to the Big House.

At the county jail, the hooliganz were thrown into another cold holding cell. It was there that they waited another hour, before they were processed and booked, and relocated to another section of the building, where they went before the circuit judge, via video. A couple of state appointed public defenders represented the crew during their initial court arraignments, and they got the shock of their lives.

"Post bail?" Lil Eddie was the first to speak on what was discussed, during the video court appearance, between the judge and the public defenders.

The public defender explained to him that now, as a newly adjudicated minor being direct filed as an adult, their adult status paired with their criminal charges made him eligible for bail. It was their first offense as adjudicated adult status.

"We can muthafucking bond outta here?" Jamir said in disbelief. Then he demanded a phone call at once.

The Hooliganz Crime Game had struck again.

"It's a miracle," muttered Vontay. He was sweating bullets he was so nervous, thinking that it was all a trick and the Feds were about to surely rain on their parade.

Many of them were thinking along those same lines. Then, when it was time for them to leave, after LaShonda and Anya posted bail for them all, Peanut cried like a bitch, thinking it was over for them.

"This gotta be a dream," Jamir said, once he stepped foot out of the jailhouse and laid eyes on his mother,

LaShonda was crying as she rushed into her son's arms and squeezed him for dear life. Then Jamir looked over her shoulder to see Harmoni standing there, looking like she was about to bust. One look at his girl and Jamir knew this was far from a dream.

Then he stepped into Harmoni's arms.

"I miss you so much, bae. But I love you more." Jamir whispered in her ear, as he reached down and placed a hand upon her bloated belly.

"I love you, too," she smiled into his eyes. And then her smile suddenly transformed into a look of instant fright.

"What is it?" He looked worried.

Harmoni looked down and he followed her gaze. When he saw the wetness seeping along the front of her pants, he knew her water had broken. Then came the first painful contraction of the labor cycle. Jamir panicked, and straight to the hospital they went. Harmoni was about to drop that load.

Jamir was about to be a father.

Chapter 24

Two Weeks Later

Toby was rolling up her White Owl at the kitchen table, preparing to meet up with Thicc Eye. She had two kilos of coke that she had to drop off in Havana. She hated going over there. Them fools out there were hot and didn't know how to move. But Thicc Eye's trap was moving a kilo a week. Plus, he had someone in Koon Bottom that paid good for two bricks on a weekly basis.

Toby sold bricks for twenty thousand dollars, but if she had to make the drop, it was an additional three thousand dollars. Thicc Eye knew the rules and honored them. She already had the two kilos in a gym bag on the kitchen counter beside her.

Lighting the blunt and taking a long pull from it, Toby exhaled a stream of weed smoke into the air. She then snatched her car keys off the table and the gym bag off the counter. She was en route to the front door when, all of a sudden, an incoming call from her phone vibrated in her front pocket. She paused and reached for it to see who was calling.

"What's up, Tilly?" she greeted her female cousin.

"My nigga, turn to the news wherever you at," said Tilly in an excited voice.

"I'm on my way out to run the ball, cuz. Can't you tell me what it is?" Toby exited her condo and locked the door behind her.

"Well," said Tilly.

"Somebody done kidnapped the daughter and grandson of Federal Judge Magdalena Harrington, last night. The feds are all over that shit now. So whatever you got going on right now, you need to shut it down."

Toby skidded to a halt.

"We don't got shit to do wit' that," she replied. "Why should we be worried?"

"I know, cuz. We don't got shit to do wit' it. But that won't stop them crackers from fuckin' wit' the team. Think about it," said Tilly. "Judge Harrington was sittin' on the HCG case, when they went up before her. HCG got one of the biggest, latest indictments, and their connection to Hev could link to Royal Mafia. So, we gotta cover all our bases and play everything by ear, cuz."

With a nod of understanding, Toby said, "You are so right, cuz. Thanks for the heads up."

"That's what I'm here for."

Toby made her way out of the building and into her duck-off ride, a money green TansAm with five percent tint. She got into traffic and went to make her drop-offs. Once she handled this business, she was closing up shop at all her trap spots. Thirty minutes later, she was on her way back to Quincy with sixty-seven thousand dollars contained in a knapsack. By this time, the Royal Mafia crew was already on point with the kidnap, and was moving with caution.

Nothing was going to steal the show.

Life was too good.

But just to make sure everything was really good, Toby decided to stop by all her trap spots to see for herself. She was chief of the drug trade dealings in her camp. It was her responsibility to make sure her business was secured. The Show Quarters spot was shut down and executed, as her workers were now cleaning up the place to rid it of anything that would get them caught. Kareesha, Tiara and Dreka were on top of the game, as usual.

The next location was over in High Bridge, where Andrea was already done closing up shop and outside, trimming the hedges in front of the house. The other two, India and Myrical, were already gone, and clear of their duties.

"What you got goin on, Drea?" Toby asked. She had to yell over the sound of the roaring, gas-operated saw trimmers. "You know what the hell you're doing?"

Drea, who was the latest recruit, had solidified her position as a trapper. She was not only a go-getter, but skilled in the hand-to-hand combat department, and a great conversationalist. But here it was, she was outside trimming the hedges out front, with safety goggles on and gloves, like she was accustomed to this type of work. To Toby, this was something her Uncle Pete would be doing, not a woman, and it was damn sure unexpected of a Royal Mafia member.

Shutting off the machine and finishing up, Drea looked up at her and said, "This is what I do, Toby. I like to keep my shit nice and well-groomed."

"You know I got people who'll do this type of stuff for a little or nothin'? Said Toby.

"Why pay when I can do it on my own?"

"Suit yourself," Toby replied. "I just stopped by to see if everything was good on your end."

"Yeah. I got it all under control. But can I asked you a serious question, Toby?"

"Sure."

Andrea seemed very thoughtful for a second. "Besides all the street shit and stuff, what're your true aspirations in life, Toby? I mean, like your ultimate goals and dreams?"

Now she really had Toby looking at her meaningfully, knowing how deep Drea could get at times. Some of the other Royals thought she just wanted to know too much from her endless questions, but that was her personality. Drea just wanted to go with a person on an intellectual level.

"You know what's crazy, Drea? All I know is thuggin' and gettin' to the bag. I never really thought about nothin' other than my survival in these streets."

"So, you plan on doing this the rest of your life?"

Toby hesitated with her reply.

"No. You don't. Maybe there's something you really care about doin' that your pride and thoughts of what others might think of you is stoppin' you from doing. I know there's at least one thing, Toby. Just give me one thing," persisted Andrea, seeing the wheels turning in Toby's head, through her eyes.

Out of nowhere, approached a crack head by the name of Cornbread. In his hand, he clutched his money, apparently, looking for his fix. This was one of Toby's favorite customers back when she and Delani were trappin' together.

"Look who's found ha'self back in the slums wit' the rest of us." Cornbread cracked a crooked smile, revealing dark black gums and several missing and stained teeth.

"What's up Cornbread?"

"You, Toby. Been missin' you around da way, it ain't been the same since you and Dee been gone," he said.

"What, my girls ain't taking care of y'all, over in Pepper Hill?"

"Who? LeLe and 'nem?" Cornbread frowned and shook his head.

"The dope ain't the same, Toby. Not like it is over here, it ain't," he said.

"The fuck you mean the dope ain't the same? I'm the one who cooked that shit up, Cornbread. It's all the same."

"Like I said, it's not the same. Can I get a forty piece for thirty-five, missy?" Cornbread directed his attention to Andrea, who, without saying a word, reached down into the front of her pants and fiddled in there for a second.

Toby was puzzled and doubtful.

Seconds later, Cornbread was skipping away with his product, as Toby watched after him, her thoughts conflated by the prospect of her money being tampered with.

"I don't like this shit, Drea. I know ain't nothing wrong wit' my dope. I rocked that shit up myself." Toby whipped out her cell phone and Andrea stilled her hand.

"Humble yourself. Calm down. Breathe." Andrea's voice was soft and reassuring, and Toby looked at her quietly.

"If what he said is true, then there is an explanation for it," Toby said. "I'm about to hurt me a bitch."

"It's okay, Toby. Don't be so quick to jump to conclusions, before finding out the reason why. Go investigate and see how you can rectify the problem. I know what?" Andrea picked up her lawn care machine and said, "Lemme put this stuff up and I'll go wit' you over there."

With an exhaled breath, Toby nodded her head. "A'ight." There was always something or another that seemed to not go as one hoped it should.

Maybe Drea was right, thought Toby. *I really do need to find out what my aspirations are other than all this street shit. Something gotta give.*

Chapter 25

The Hooliganz Crime Gang's numbers had climbed up to twenty-one numbers, with Jamir and White Boy Ty heading the organization. While Jamir was focused on fatherhood, Ty and Hollow were making the moves to keep the crew a certified camp.

Born nine pounds, seven ounces, Jamaal Romell had become Jamir's main priority. It was such a sensational experience that Jamir found himself floating on Cloud 9. Ursula, who was Harmoni's grandmother and mentor, was hard on Jamir about standing firm on his duties as a father. The young hooligan was approaching his seventeenth birthday, and he had major plans. It was going to be a movie, and Jamaal would be the star.

There was nothing at that moment more important to Jamir than being there for his son.

Family was important to him.

Something so powerful was happening to Jamir in the wake of his son's arrival. He was having thoughts of actually retiring from the streets to build a sheltered life around Jamaal. But his money was looking funny, and he needed to reach financial stability, before taking on that decision.

"So, what do you wanna do, son?" asked his stepfather, Tony, whom Jamir loved and respected, as though he was his true biological father.

"Know what I really want?" Jamir and Tony were weaving through traffic, just vibing, after making a few errands in town for their demanding ladies. "I wanna be a club owner," he said. "But I also wanna start something like a Boys and Girls Club around here. I wanna give back to the community."

"That's an admirable thing to do. But a club, though? You know that's eventually going to get you involved back in the streets."

"I know how to separate the two, Tony. I'm about business."

"If you say so," Tony sighed deeply.

"You don't think I can do it?" asked Jamir. Then he looked up and zeroed in on a McDonald's restaurant coming up ahead, and hit the blinkers. "I'ma show you what I'm capable of," he continued, and made the turn into the entrance.

"You don't have to prove anything to me, son." Tony then looked up to see where they were going. "Just pay attention."

Jamir entered the fast food restaurant and demanded to speak with its manager. What he was about to do was something he read about in a book he once read in Horizons Bookstore & Lounge one day. Tony walked into the restaurant, just as the manager, whose name was T. Parker, showed up on the scene.

"Is there a problem, Jamir?" asked the wide-bodied manager.

"So you know me?" Jamir was astonished. Tiffany Parker was her name, and yes, she knew him. Her cousin was Lil LuLu. At the mention of his hooligan brotha, Jamir became instantly dismal for a split second.

"What time is it?" Jamir replied.

"It's going on one o'clock, why?" said Tony.

"A'ight, Tiffany, how much would it cost me to rent out the restaurant for the whole afternoon?" Asked Jamir.

"That's somethin' I have to consult wit' my boss on, Jamir. I mean, what exactly are you tryna do?"

"I'm tryna feed the children of our community."

His statement astounded her. Tiffany said she knew a plan that just might work. Tony was intrigued by this, and watched as the two put their heads together. Their energies then led them to the manager's office, where the plot thickened.

"I got fifteen hundred to invest in this," Jamir said, once they had reached a mutual understanding, where money would be concerned. Tiffany nodded and reached for a calculator to do the math that was needed to begin the mission.

"This is gonna be a whole lot of Happy Meals and, I must say, Jay, you got a good thing goin' on," said Tony.

That afternoon, children from all over Godsden County would come and get themselves a Happy Meal. Quincy was a small, black town, whose whole existence consisted of poverty, AIDS infestation, low education, and some of the most dangerous individuals that ever lived. A lot of kids went to bed hungry at night, all because their so-called mothers would spend their money on drugs, hair weave, and designer nails, mothers whose priories were extremely fucked up. Then they wondered why the children turned out to be like Trill, Spud, or even Deff Jam Booby. They all were once kids, who lived so poorly that their fear of starving to death turned them into young barbarians with no consistency.

So, if Jamir could make this work, it would give the youth of their community hope.

Shamar was once hopeless and just as unfortunate as those Jamir was aiming to help. If it wasn't for his hooliganz crew, the originals, and his late, dear auntie, Shamar would have probably turned out worse than he had.

Jamir understood the struggle, and he wanted to show his people that he wasn't afraid to show he cared. He was down for them. He was devoted to them. But little did he know, the troubles that were heading his way because of it.

Then the called up his HCG team and got them involved. This was their moment.

"Please tell me you got some McNuggets in the mix, too," said Zamon, when he got there and was told the plan.

Several of the others reacted to this, too.

McNuggets were now in the mix. And Jamir had to agree, for the nuggets were one of his favorites, as well.

Chapter 26

At that very moment, Dejah was walking back to the cell from her lawyer/client visit. She had mixed emotions about everything she'd learned today, especially after what she was now about to be forced to do on her own. She knew who her rodent was, and he had to die.

Kahlil had to die. His betrayal was punishable by death.

A little over a week ago, after the hooliganz had beat the system by manipulating their own freedom, Jamir had contacted Dejah in regard to what Lil One told him. At first, Dejah wasn't tryna hear that it was actually Kahlil who ratted them out. But when Jamir vowed to locate Booty Boo and get her side of the story, Dejah encouraged him to do so.

In the process, Dejah pressured her lawyer to find out who the confidential informant was. If anything, their statements had to be documented in whatever transcripts that were of substantial importance. Today, her lawyer had given her a name, the very same name that had been haunting her consciousness. And just two days ago, Jamir had confirmed Booty Boo's story as being comparable with Lil One's accusations. Now Dejah had her man, and he would suffer for his sins.

Back at her housing unit, Dejah was just in time for the second afternoon count time walk-through. While all the women were headed to their cells for the hour count, Dejah beckoned Shoo Baby over to her small cell. Shoo Baby was still in the day room area, sitting down at one of several tables, studying the Chessboard in front of her. Ever since she'd learned how to play the game, she'd pretty much challenged everybody who dared to put up with her aggressiveness and impatient demeanor. Just yesterday, she lost five games straight, and the victor, an Irish woman, who went by the name of Roselyn, thought it was okay to clown Shoo Baby about it. Shoo Baby laid her right out on the dayroom floor. Today, it was Vera Mae Walters, a seventy year old, no nonsense, seasoned gangstress, who'd been incarcerated for nearly forty years for a list of violent crimes. The old female convict was still feisty, at her age, but she was also patient and understanding of someone like Shoo Baby, and somehow managed to keep the hooligan focused.

It was very challenging to keep Shoo Baby focused and settled down long enough to watch her flourish.

At her superior's beck, Shoo Baby excused herself and stepped around the table to help the older woman up before she left to go see what Dejah wanted.

"How was your visit wit' your lawyer?"

Dejah replied, "Progressive." Then she nodded for Shoo Baby to step into the cell for a second. Mookie was laid back on her bed, reading a book by Leila Motely called *Night Crawling*.

"Everything good?" Mookie asked.

"No," said Dejah.

"Kahlil is our rat, ladies. It was just confirmed by Nancy Logan, saw it in Black and white."

"Damn," was all Shoo Baby could say as she dropped her head in total disbelief.

Dejah explained quickly what she wanted, and assured them that she would see to it.

After Shoo Baby took her leave, Dejah told Mookie to prepare the phone for an emergency phone call to her fellow incarcerated hooliganz.

"But wait 'til after the guards walk by," said Dejah. She then removed her shoes and pulled over her uniform shirt to expose her well-muscled torso. The T-Shirt she had on underneath was tight fitting, as her luscious titties threatened to bust through the fabric. Dejah laid down until the guards made the walk-through, fifteen minutes later. When the cell phone was brought out and hooked up, there were eight missed calls and eleven messages, all from her loved ones and business associates.

She called Delani.

"Merge Shamar and LJ in too," Dejah told her young hooligan, the second he answered the phone.

"LJ's out on work duty as the house man, but I got Mar wit' me right now," said Delani, a minute later.

"What's good, cuz?" Shamar replied humbly. Since his incarceration, he'd been on some real deal scholar shit, reading law books and the Holy Koran.

"Besides LJ, this I'm bout to express to you goes nowhere else. Am I clean?"

"Yeah."

"I gotchu."

"Okay." Dejah took a deep breath. "I found out who our Master Splinter is, y'all. It's Mr. Two Step Shawty." She was sad. The name was given to Kahlil after the club one night, when Lil Durk came to Tallahassee to perform at Club Top Flighty. That night, Kahlil was so high off weed and champagne that he danced his way through the whole club event, doing the two-step rhythm to every song. The crew clowned him that night, giving him the pet name Mr. Two Step Shawty.

At hearing this, the line became quiet between Shamar and Delani. It was as if they were expecting Dejah to tell them that she was just bullshitting.

"I'm not bullshittin'," said Dejah, as if reading their minds. "I saw it all in black and white, after meetin' wit Nancy. And Dee, you know I wouldn't ask you to-"

"Just shut the hell up, Dejah," Delani replied. "I know what needs to be done. It's done. There's nothing else to fuckin' talk about on the situation."

"As a matter of fact, Delani, there is," said Dejah.

"What?"

From across the room, standing at the door, keeping watch, Mookie glanced back to meet Dejah's gaze, which read that she already knew how Delani was taking this. Kahlil was his big cousin, and after recently losing his twin brother, Delani would feel targeted somehow by the universe and was about to challenge it head on in the most violent way.

That's what Dejah was afraid of.

"You know what? I love you, Dee. That's all. Play your cards right, baby boy," said Dejah.

Delani disconnected.

That's when Dejah really began to worry.

"Please, God, you know our circumstances, you know all the shit we have to go through. But if you really fuck wit' a bitch, don't let my baby boy fuck this up. That shit'll kill us all," she said.

"Dej?"

"Yeah, Mook?" Dejah opened her eyes.

"You know you just prayed to God to conspire in helpin' Dee kill his own cousin, right?"

"I know what I just prayed for, Mookie!"

"And you're dead serious, too." Mookie seemed shocked by this and shook her head. Dejah ignored her and then proceeded to send Jamir a much needed text message.

Shit was about go down.

Kahlil was definitely living on borrowed time now. All rats must die.

Chapter 27

Delani had only been back on max since yesterday evening, when the medical administration demanded that he be removed from his cell in infirmity to someplace else. So he was brought to the confinement house unit, where all max inmates are confined in a cell twenty-three hours a day, with only one hour out to shower. But not even that was promised. There had been days many had gone without showering. Showering on max was done in odd cell numbers on one day and even numbers the following day.

However, Delani didn't care one way or the other, he never left the cell for nothing. He would rather take a bird bath in his sink than risk being cuffed behind his back and shackled just to be escorted to a shower stall. He'd witnessed and heard of many tragedies from that decision alone. Niggaz, having done some creep shit in general population, and now behind the door on max, leave their cell for the shower, only to get stabbed to death by another inmate, also weighed down in chains. What was so crazy was the cooperation of the guard escorting you. They be down with the whole lick. It was like, why get a hard-on watching prisoners kill one another.

Enough money or influence would get one's cuffs loosened enough for them to slip their hands out and get the job done. In the federal facility, if one wanted you bad enough, he would get you. It was a battlefield. You couldn't trust anyone, which was why Delani was now under

"Housed Alone" status. Because it had already been confirmed by him that if you wasn't HCG, then he wasn't sleeping in the same cell with you. His spoken threat to kill anybody who stepped foot in his cell, who he didn't want there, was taken very seriously.

Come to find out, a friend of a friend of one of the Royals had a brother-in-law that worked there, and LJ had persuaded him to fuck with them. That's how he was able to get out of his cell and work as an orderly houseman on the afternoon shifts.

His name was Richard "Spanky" McNeil, an older guy in his mid-thirties, a sergeant office on his shift, cool as a fan, but dirty, too. But LJ was seeming to work his magic with him because that was who was gonna lead him to setting Kahlil up for the kill. Might as well take advantage of the opportunity while they had the chance.

Although Kahlil was upstairs on the second tier, in the cell with Might Mouse, another loyal hooligan, Delani didn't want it to go down in the room. He couldn't see up there, and Delani wanted to witness his cousin perish. Might Mouse would surely take Khali on that gangsta ride but Delani didn't want him getting in any trouble because of it. With the pressure the hooliganz were already under from the prison war on the yard recently, it was best to chill for now.

Delani would wait it out.

"Patience is a virtue," he mumbled softly.

Right then, there was a tap on his cell door. Delani already knew who it was. He got up from the covers on his bed and went to the door. There was a white towel covering the rectangular shaped glass window in the door. When he pulled it aside, there stood LJ, serious looking and with a push-broom in his hand.

"I just saw Mar in the other wing, he said you needed to see me. LJ's voice was low and curious.

"I do," Delani answered.

"What's up?"

Another thanks to Bobby for teaching some of the hooliganz the importance of sign language, because now that lesson was very much needed at that moment.

Delani signed with letters, spelling out his message. *Just talked to Dejah. She saw Nancy. Kahlil sold us all out to the Feds. It's confirmed.*

LJ frowned. He signed back, *I'll handle it.*

Delani replied, *not yet. We wait.*

"But I want to, brah. That nigga sour," LJ said angrily.

Placing a finger to his lips, Delani responded, *this is my call. We wait. But keep it sealed. Keep doing you. Kahlil is smart. Don't act different toward him. Not now. But look for a hitta somebody trusts. No hooliganz.*

"I gotcha, my nigga," said LJ tightly.

"Focus, LJ," he replied.

He nodded.

When Delani pressed his fist against the glass window, LJ did the same, and the love was acknowledged.

It was settled. Kahlil's time was almost expired. He had to die.

Chapter 28

The drive to Pepper Hill was spent building on some growth and development shit. Andrea was persistent when it came down to the meeting of the minds. She was deep and spiritual, but most of all, the bitch was also virtual. Andrea's humbleness was not to be taken lightly. She was the quiet before the storm type of bitch. Definitely not like the other Royals, and Toby was glad she was on her team.

Once they made it to Pepper Hill, Toby was more humble now. At least that's what she started out being. She wanted some straightening, though. LeLe had some explaining to do. She was the hustler. Therefore, it was her responsibility to keep the customers happy.

The customers weren't happy.

Sitting out on the porch steps, busting down a Dutch blunt was Skarr and Erikah, but no LeLe. When Toby got out of the car, she walked right up to both, the watch-out and the shooter, then eased past them to get to the front door.

"If you looking for LeLe, she not here," said Skarr, who literally had a six inch scar going across her face, resulting from a box cutter. The person responsible was dead now, killed by her own weapon, which she used to mark her death.

"Where she at?"

"She got a call from her old man and had to leave," said Erikah, in turn.

"What is this shit I'm hearing about bad products coming from this spot?" Toby asked.

Both Skarr and Erikah looked at one another.

"I'm fuckin' right here," Toby was trying to keep her composure, but she was feeling tired right now. She was tempted to smash both of them bitches across their heads.

"I told LeLe that shit was a bad move, but she didn't want to listen to me," said Erikah.

"You still ain't tellin' me shit," Toby replied.

"It's like this," Skarr cut in. "LeLe's old man Pitt came down here the other day on some trip shit. They got into it and he ended up takin' her pack from her. Apparently, he ain't feelin' her sellin' dope for somebody other than his crude ass. She just let him take the shit, too."

"Until we made her go back and get it from him," Erikah added to the fire.

At the moment, Toby was glaring down at Skarr. Her position was to protect the trap and its product and workers. But to hear that this chump ass nigga, Pitt, had come and taken from the trap without any repercussion was lost on her.

"The nigga switched the packs wit' her and gave LeLe his beat up ass dope," said Erikah.

"LeLe scared of that pussy nigga," said Skarr.

"She used her own money to pay you, after we started gettin' complaints from the customers. She then worked off what was left of that bullshit dope, and charged the loss to the game. You got paid in full, my nigga, that's all that mattered, right? Her only concern was paying you your money."

Toby looked at Skarr as she spoke and knew that her shooter was trying to protect LeLe's honor.

"You both kept this shit from me though," Toby replied. "And that alone puts you in violation," she added.

"But I'm not gonna report this to Hev because it's my call. Plus, I got paid all my money. But what I am gonna do is get that fade from both of y'all for even allowing it to happen."

"Let's do it," Skarr said, without hesitation, standing up on her feet.

The women all went around to the back of the trap house and got busy. Toby gave them both hell, but Erikah was impressive with her hands. She was a great fighter.

Afterwards, they all embraced one another and talked for a while, tying up with a plan to deal with LeLe and Pitt.

"That's her daughter's father," said Andrea.

"And that's supposed to mean something to me, Drea?" Toby shot her a stern look, as a lump began to gradually swell up on top of her forehead.

Before Andrea could answer that, the sound of Toby's cell phone rang. She retrieved her phone and saw that it was her little brotha Jamir.

"What it do, main man?"

"It's poppin' over here at Micky D's sis. You need to pull up, like right now. Get over here," he said.

"What's going on Jay?"

"Just get here, Toby. I need your help."

Without having to be told again, Toby rushed to her car, with Andrea on her heels. Skarr told Erikah to lock up the trap, then took off after them for the car.

Minutes later, they pulled up in the entrance of McDonald's downtown and was surprised at what they saw. Dozens and dozens of school kids were all over the place, eating Happy Meals and McNuggets and laughing and playing. The Hooliganz Crime Gang crew were passing out food to the children from every entrance of the building.

"The hell is that?" When Toby realized she had no place to park, due to the numerous school kids crowding the parking lot area, she just parked her car right there in the middle of the lot and got out.

"Bout time yo ass showed up," said Kweli, handing out Happy Meals to children.

"Help me pass these shits out."

"For real?" Toby was shoved forward and to the side by children, who were running all around the place and bumping into her. Instinct made her reach for her tool, until she realized that it was just kids acting a fool.

"What happen to your face?" A young boy with his two front teeth missing asked with mischievous eyes.

"The same thang bout to happen to yours, if you don't get your little bad ass outta my face."

"Shut up. Punk. You got beat up. Ah-ha," the boy laughed, punching her on the hip, and took off running,

"No. Stop, silly." White Boy Ty wrapped an arm around Toby's shoulders, just as she was about to chase after the child and dump him on his head.

"He's just a kid," he said.

It was a riot out there.

Then White Boy Ty kissed her on the lump atop of her forehead and grinned. Then he just walked away, without another word, making Toby stare after him in silent wonder at his audacity for what he just did.

Suddenly, a group of young girls giggled and gave Toby funny faces because of what they had just witnessed. Toby gave them the middle finger. She was even surprised that it made her blush, too. And then she went to go help her hooliganz change lives, just by providing one simple meal.

She had never done anything like this before, giving back to the community. And she felt damn good about it. A damn good start.

Chapter 29

A hunted animal develops a sense of when something isn't quite right at all. Maybe a sound, or the absence of one, or something from the corner of the eye that wasn't there a minute ago causes alarm. Maybe it's a word, a facial expression, or a glimpse of an injury that tips them off.

Heaven had a sense, when the woman walked into the bar and claimed the spot across from the busy bartender.

The woman wasn't one of the regulars, not one of the pathetic tricks that were always lingering around the bar, looking for johns to serve up. Her clothes were evidence of their own brand, a new Autumn Adeigbo Camile dress, expensive six-inch heroes, the color of auburn. Her skin was golden tanned, almost perfect, as if she had just left a tanning salon.

From her vantage point near the back of the bar, Heaven could see that the mysterious woman was watching attentively what was going on around her through the large mirror positioned behind the bar upon the wall.

"What will it be, boss lady?" Asked June, the bartender, who swiftly appeared before her with a dish towel hanging over his meaty right shoulder.

"Just a Coke will do, sir. Thank you."

"A Coke?" June gave her a questioning glance.

"And a couple of questions, when you have time," she replied, and removed a pack of Salem's from her mink coat pocket. She shook out a cigarette and June leaned over to light it for her.

"One Coke coming up, Miss Lady," he said.

"It's Debra," she replied. "Debra Moretti. And you are?" She took a drag from her cigarette and blew out a smoke ring with perfect practice.

"Junebug. But e'erbody call me June." The bartender slid a glass of Coca-Cola across the counter to her.

"Thank you, June," she said with such politeness.

"You're not from around here, so what brings you to the smallest parts of such a great big world. Debra?"

"Hunting."

Her reply gave him pause. "Huntin' season ain't till another four months, so what're you huntin' this early?"

"Different prospects, of course."

"Such as?" June snuck a quick glance in Heaven's direction and she gave him the signal to keep her talking.

Heaven had already spoken to Rikah, and her shooter was now in position, as well as the other three Royals occupying the room.

It was then that Debra opened her mink coat and revealed that she was indeed equipped with a shoulder holster and a chrome automatic pistol inside. But it was inside the coat pocket where she withdrew a King of Spades, playing card. That same card she then slid towards June and he picked it up.

"I am looking for him," she said.

"I'm confused, Miss Lady."

"The king of this town, June. Stay with me, darling, because it gets better as you go." She smiled innocently.

"Are we speaking streetwise or-"

"Exactly, June. The streets, who is its King?" Her piercing gray-blue eyes bore into him and June suddenly found himself captivated by their essence for a moment.

"There is no king of the streets here, in this town, Debra. You came to the wrong place for that," said June.

"How disappointing," she pretended to pout.

"But we do have a queen, tho," he added

The mysterious woman named Debra's eyes lit up. "How intriguing. And who might that be, June?"

"Depends on who's tryna know," replied Heaven, just behind the woman's ear, and Debra stiffened. Discreetly, June had given the signal that she was armed, and Heaven, along with her Royals, moved in for the kill, if need be.

Glancing in the mirror behind her, Debra spotted four women, having suddenly advanced upon her. She quickly recovered from being startled and spun around slowly in her seat.

A smirk appeared on the woman's face.

"Debra Moretti, former matriarch of the Moretti family, based out of Newark, New Jersey. And you are?" She asked.

"And I am Queen Hev, matriarch of the Royal Mafia Family. And you are now on my turf," said Heaven.

"Royal Mafia, eh? I like that," said Debra. Then a very curious expression appeared on her matured face.

"Before you even say it, yes, I am young, but I'm also perfectly fit for such a position. Now please state your intentions, because I don't take too kindly of strange people coming up in my establishment to inquire about who I am."

"A partnership," said Debra.

"A partnership, what aspect are we talking?" Heaven replied.

"One that will cure all your worries and make you a very happy woman," Debra Moretti said.

"What makes you think I have any worries?" Heaven asked.

"We all worry about something or another, Hev."

Heaven replied. "And what are yours?"

"I only have one worry."

"Which is?"

"You, Heaven. Not being able to repay you and Marlon back for what he did to save me and my family."

"My father?" Heaven looked at her strangely.

"Yes. Your father. A very fine man, a man of great valor and patience. Marlon Jones," said Debra. "You have his eyes as well, Hev. That's why I am here to return the favor."

"How do you know my father?" Heaven asked.

"It's a long story, love."

Heaven climbed onto the barstool next to the woman and said, "I got time for a story."

And boy what a story it was, a story that led to the truth of Marlon Jones' survival, and his resurrection. A life after his acclaimed death, and now the betrayal that was about to lead to a massive destruction.

"I was there that night at that bar in Georgia," Debra told Heaven what she had witnessed and then proceeded to show her very own recording of Marlon's abduction.

Heaven was totally heartbroken.

"He would have wanted you to know the truth, Hev. This is proof. And your father is the real true reason you're still free right now, to avenge his death," said Debra.

There were tears in Heaven's eyes as she sat thinking about how he had been betrayed. A dark rage was building inside of her. She wanted blood, and blood she would get.

Chapter 30

Kevin Gates "Power" was playing in the background and White Boy Ty and Toby had just finished burning her second blunt. Ever since that kiss, three days ago, in McDonald's parking lot, something between them had awakened, and it felt right. Today he had called and told her that he was pullin' up on her to chill. He had come through later that afternoon, like he said he would. After being granted to bust that pussy open something viciously, they lounged around in her queen sized bed and were chillin'.

Toby couldn't front though, they shared something special, and she had always thought Ty was truly official for a white boy. Things between them were really starting to feel like they should have made this move. However, she didn't wanna jinx shit by getting all hopeful too soon. Toby was tryna play the shit cool and be humble about it. But she was really feeling White Boy Ty. They were so much alike. And he wasn't her man yet, although Toby wasn't sure if that's what he really, truly wanted. A part of her did, but then there was that other part that made her unsafe. It made her scared.

She wasn't actually scared of Ty, only what she would do to him, if he tried to play her like a pawn. Toby would go ballistic on his white ass, for real.

Ty had a mean fuck game and he ate the pussy and ass like fresh groceries. He knew how to treat a real bitch. She knew, without a doubt, that she could really fall for his ass. And that shit had Toby on edge, almost nervous.

Toby was having mixed feelings. She was not sure if it was her heart, her head, or her snatching tight pussy talking, but whichever it was, she knew, if she gave in to the feelings that were gradually growing inside of her and Ty turned out to be on some fuck shit, shit was gonna get real drastic for him. Her gut told her Ty was a good man, with good intentions, where her heart was concerned, but what she didn't know was whether he cheated on bitches or not. She never really knew for him to have women he was committed to, but she knew he was indeed attractive for a white boy, and his swag game was on point. He could probably snatch any bitch he wanted.

Just the thought of White Boy Ty being with another woman made her trigger finger itch. She was fucked up 'bout his white ass. He was that dude.

As long as they kept shit the way it was now, there should be no stress and no pressure. She was playing her position, so now Ty had to do his part.

If only he knew the diamond in the rough, which was now in his possession.

"What're you thinking about, Toby?" White Boy Ty leaned forward to kiss the top of her newly re-twisted locs, as she laid her head upon his naked chest.

"On whether I should kill you now or later."

He laughed. "You serious?"

"I don't wanna be hurt, Ty," she replied with earnest.

"I don't plan to, my love. C'mere." Ty tapped her on the shoulder and then guided her up to straddle his lap, so she could look into his eyes.

"I'll never hurt you, Toby. My word. I've been checking for you since day one, years ago. I just didn't know how you would feel if I had told you how I felt."

"You shoulda said something," she replied.

"I thought it'll be good to just love you from a distance, instead of how I really wanted to. But that changed the other day, after I saw that you was hurt."

"I wasn't hurt." She rolled her eyes down at him.

"You had that lump on your head, Toby."

"That shit wasn't nothing."

"Well it was to me," White Boy Ty said, pulling her forehead down so that he could kiss it once again, right where the lump had finally gone down, but left a bruise to remind them that it was there.

"I just wanna make you happy, Toby. Real shit, my nigga."

When Toby opened her mouth to say something, the ring of her phone stopped her. She wanted to ignore it, but something told her that she should answer it instead.

"Hold on Ty." She climbed off him to reach her ringing cell phone on top of the mahogany night able.

"Geloo?"

"It's up right now, Toby. You need to get to the headquarters, like yesterday," said Baiyina in an excited tone.

"What's going on?" Toby asked, alarmed.

"It's about to go down, sis. It's war time."

"With who?" Demanded Toby.

Baiyina paused for a moment. "Wit' the Hooliganz Crime Gang," she said.

Toby felt her heart skip a beat. Then she turned her gaze on the person lying in her bed.

"What?" Ty asked.

Toby reached for her gun. It was war.

Chapter 31

Jamir was stretched out on the living room sofa of his and Harmoni's gated community home, out at Promise Land Estates, a fairly recently constructed landscape, filled with beautiful houses out in the Midway area. Lying on top of his chest, sound asleep, was his son, Jamaal. All he seemed to want to do was eat, sleep and shit his diaper, like it was a new trend or something. But Jamir was game, he was all for it. Even though, baby boy kept them up all times of night, that was just more reason for Jamir to spend time with him.

Harmoni thought her man was becoming obsessed with his son, never giving her much time to get fully comfortable with Jamaal, before he took him away. The occurrence had become both frustrating and admirable. It was as if Jamir feared he would be taken away from his son, at some point, and was just trying to get as much father/son time as he could, while he still could.

The reality of it all kinda scared Harmoni, too, figuring Jamir knew something vital that she didn't know.

His constant presence was fulfilling.

Jamir was changing. He was changing for the better, for the greater good, where Jamaal's well-being was concerned.

That was being a father, being honorable.

When the baby was carefully lifted off his chest. Jamir's eyes snapped open and he sat up at once. Harmoni told him to chill out, that she was only going to lay Jamaal down in his baby crib. He relaxed and settled back on the sofa, reaching for his phone on the coffee table.

No sooner than his hand grasped the phone and pulled it to him, the front door reputed with a startling boom of a forced impact from the other side. Jamir stiffened in sudden surprise. Then, a spilt second later, the door exploded inwardly and a team of armed Royals filed through it.

"The fuck?" Jamir shot to his feet and Meesha, the first one through the door, knocked him back down, with a blow to the chest by the stock of her assault rifle.

Two more Royals, Lil Bit and Pumpkin, both armed with semi-automatics, roughed Jamir up a little, before taking ahold of him and dragging him towards the front door.

"Jay!" Harmoni rushed up front and skidded to a halt.

Meesha upped her AK-47 and aimed it dead at Harmoni's face, saying, "I'll kill your ass, if you take one more step, bitch."

In the back room, Jamaal started wailing.

With caution in her eyes, Harmoni lifted her hands in surrender and quickly retreated to comfort her son. She cast a worried glance over her shoulder and disappeared.

Meanwhile, Jamir was struggling against the two Royals and trying to fight back, only to get assaulted further with the weapons. Standing outside the dark minivan idling at the curb was Tap Tap, also armed and dangerous, and ready to murk something.

"You keep on resisting and I'm just gon' shoot you, Jay," Tap Tap announced in a threatening tone.

"Why y'all doin' this? Where is Hev? Where my sista?" he stressed before being punched in his mouth. The blow had come from Meesha and it dazed him momentarily. The bitch hit like a man.

Together, the two Royals shoved Jamir into the minivan, as Tap Tap and Meesha hurried and got to the front. At the feet of the two Royals, lying on the floor, Jamir was bleeding profusely from his nose and mouth. The minivan had no rear seats, just an open space in the back, preferably for large cargo, and he was that cargo.

As the minivan got into traffic, Jamir wretched his brain for a reason why the Royals were kidnapping him. Was Heaven behind the move? He thought to himself.

"Hev sent y'all at me?" Jamir asked in distress.

"Shut the fuck up, Jamir," Meesha spoke from the front passenger seat, her cold brown eyes seeming to glow in the dark.

One thing Jamir did know was that the plan was not to kill him, at least not at the moment. And if this was Heaven's doing, then the mission would be for him to be brought to her. Whatever she had in her heart, Heaven would see that it got done personally, herself.

Jamir thought about his son, still hearing his potent cries in his conscience, scared that he wouldn't see him again. Jamir was also grateful, despite the circumstances, that Harmoni and his son did not get hurt in the process.

He saw the pair of headlights flash on the minivan, illuminating the inside. Then, a split second later, Jamir felt himself being jolted violently into Pumpkin's legs, at the unsuspected impact of the two vehicles colliding into each other brought everything to a startling halt. Jamir groaned in agony, as he felt Pumpkin now lying on top of him. Moments later, automatic rounds rang out as fearful cries of the Royals were heard over the chaos being created inside.

Jamir knew what was happening, but by whom exactly, he had no clue, only that the Royals were all being murdered and the hit had him kinda shook.

"Jay?" Toby suddenly yelled.

From beneath Pumpkin's dead body, Jamir only grunted in response, as he heard the side door of the minivan slide open.

"He's under her," White Boy Ty's voice was heard next.

As he laid there in discomfort, Jamir felt the dead weight of Pumpkin being pulled from atop of him. Then he sat up, like the Undertaker, and looked at his brother from another mother.

"We gotta go, Jay," he said.

"Gotta get back to the house, Ty," said Jamir.

"Then let's go." Toby slapped the bullet riddled body of the minivan anxiously, as Jamir was helped outside.

Once he was back on his feet, Jamir looked at Ty's car and saw that it was totaled. He then shifted his gaze towards home, and took off running in its direction. Both Toby and White Boy Ty ran after him, all the way to his house.

By the time Jamir ran the four streets over, he heard Jamaal still crying inside miserably from the front porch. Harmoni had managed to shut the damaged front door to keep away any more unwanted individuals. Jamir pounded a fist against the door and called out to Harmoni to open it. He thought twice about busting through the already ruined door, for fear of Harmoni shooting him in the process. Because he knew the first chance she got, she went for one of the guns that he had hidden around the house.

Harmoni snatched the front door open at once.

"Oh, Jay," she cried, while standing there clutching a black .9mm pistol in her right hand. Without a word, Jamir rushed past her for his crying son and lifted him up from the baby carrier on the sofa chair.

"Go pack up, quickly," he told his baby mama. Harmoni didn't even give him a verbal response. She went to go do as she was told.

Fifteen minutes later, they were all driving around the murder scene, which had brought out multiple spectators. There were about twelve people standing around the gruesome sight.

"There's one more at the entrance too," said Toby. She was referring to the sentry at the gatehouse entrance of the estate, which Jamir saw and rolled right past them.

"The fuck is goin' on?" Muttered Jamir.

"It's Hev, brah. She knows," Toby answered.

"Knows what?"

"About Marlon," she said.

"She knows how he really died that night, and now she's going after everybody who was involved."

When he heard this, Jamir cussed under his breath, already knowing how this whole situation would turn out. It was war indeed.

But how did Heaven find out? Who dropped the bomb? Thought Jamir as he stressed over the matter.

Heaven was seeking revenge. At all costs.

Chapter 32

The silence was staggering. It filled the room, expanding, growing larger and larger, until Heaven squeezed the trigger of her aimed pistol. Boom. The blast was followed by the hollow-point slug exiting the chamber and slamming through the side of Redd's head, blowing her brains out the other side.

Debra Morett stilled herself at the sight of such maliciousness, as she watched Redd's body fall sideways, from the impact, and hit the floor, with a thud. Out of the corner of her eyes, she spotted Rikah slowly retreating from the room. Then Heaven commanded everybody's attention, when she suddenly spun on her heels and aimed that same pistol at Andrea's head.

"I know Redd was your girl and your loyalty was wit' her. Therefore, you are-"

"Guilty by association?" Said Andrea, cutting her off. She was far from scared, at that point, but it was obvious that she felt crossed as well. "I made a vow to you, and I will stand on that. Killing me would only prove that you are also blind to the fact that I'm a real bitch, and that I'll be just another one of your regrets, when in actuality, I'm the one who detected your real truth."

"How so?"

"For starters, Rikah," she said.

Heaven paused at the statement.

"What do you mean?"

"Rikah, in heart, is HCG through and through, no matter where she stood in this organization. Because if she wasn't, then why did she sneak outta here just now, after you killed Redd? I'll tell you why. Because she is loyal to Hooliganz Crime Gang, and now she sees you as a threat to her well-being," Andrea replied. "Now your girls are your enemies."

At that moment, everybody looked around the big room of the warehouse and Rikah was nowhere in sight. When Heaven saw this, she ordered two of her Royals to go find Rikah and bring her back.

Now Heaven was angry, especially after reconsidering Rikah's loyalty earlier and deciding against killing her. She was Shamar's recruit and they were true friends. But now Heaven was regretting her decision to keep her alive. Rikah indeed was a serious threat. She knew too much, enough to crumble the entire organization, if she wanted to. Since she was crowned queen, Heaven had entrusted everything with Rikah, not knowing this situation would ever arise.

"Still," Heaven turned her attention back to Andrea, "I need to be reassured that I can trust you further, Drea."

"There's a way that can happen."

"I'm listening."

"Russian Roulette," said Andrea. "You ever heard of the term?" She held Heaven's gaze intensely.

"I'm familiar with the term, yes."

"Right then, Baiyina stepped forward with her .357 revolver and dumped all the bullets out into the palm of her hand. Then she replaced one live round into the cylinder and spun it readily.

"I want three tries," said Andrea.

"If I live past all three, then you got me and my loyalty for life. You already know where we stand, if I don't make it."

From where she stood nearby, Debra watched with anticipation as Heaven retrieved the gun from Baiyina and put it against Andrea's forehead. She held her breath and watched Heaven's trigger finger pressing the trigger.

Click.

"I love this shit," said Andrea.

Another spin of the cylinder and Heaven said, "Are you afraid, Drea? Huh?" She put the gun politely against her head.

Andrea shrugged and replied, "I'm Royal Mafia."

Click.

"That's two," whispered Andrea.

Heaven admired her bravery and repositioned the gun, after it was spun for the third time. But she saw the bullet with her own eyes, and to her surprise, Andrea's luck had found favor in the Russian roulette game. So she did not wait anymore unnecessary time, and squeezed the trigger.

Click.

Debra let out a long breath and had to admit to herself that the experience made her nervous.

With a cocky smirk on her face, Andrea stared Heaven in her eyes and said, "I win."

"I know," Heaven said as she handed over the revolver back to Baiyina.

"Loyalty for life, right?"

"For life," said Andrea.

"Good."

Boom.

The slug from Heaven's Glock still found its mark through Andrea's forehead and opened up the back of her head, spraying blood and brain matter all over the place. Heaven didn't even blink as she took Andrea's life.

"Thank you for your loyalty," she said, staring down at the dead body of the woman she had once admired. But Heaven wasn't taking the risk of sparing Andrea's life, when she really felt some type of way about her killing the very same bitch, who once saved her life, in prison.

Moments later, Gucci and Dyamond and KeKe came back into the warehouse with bad news. Rikah had gotten away. She was nowhere to be found.

"It's all good," Heaven said.

"That makes two of the Royals on our hit list right now."

"Two?" Debra spoke up.

"Rikah and Toby. They are two HCG originals. Okay. Now we gon' take it to all of 'em. I shouldn't have to tell y'all how to handle y'all's business." Heaven turned to face the whole team of Royals, minus the ones who were dead, and the ones who were now targeted. There were a total of twenty-four of them. They were about to rain hell down all over the area, as they sought out and murdered the HCG crew.

"Are you sure this is wise, Hev?" asked Debra, once they were back on the road. "I mean, the heat that's about to come from this will jeopardize everything."

"I must avenge a part in it," said Heaven.

"She's the one who pulled the trigger, not your brothers. So I'm asking you to reconsider your strategy of retaliation. The last thing we need is a war and-"

"You shoulda thought about all that shit before you showed up, Debra. So if you're gonna continue to question my authority, I can put your ass out, right now. Then you can take your concerns and your hope for my future some-muthafuckin-where else," Heaven replied, glaring to her side, as the other woman sat in the backseat beside her.

With a deep sigh, Debra shook her head and said, "Okay. If it's war you want, at least let me utilize my own men. That way, your Royals and your position won't be exposed?"

"What men?"

"As the former matriarch of my own Italian crime family, I'm proud to say that there's quite a few goons who still behold my love and honor," said Debra.

"And where are they?" she asked.

"Closer than you'll ever know, Hev. Since we met back at the bar, my men have been following my every step, in discretion. All it takes is one phone call," Debra assured her.

If only one could see the astonished look on Heaven's face at the moment. "So, you're saying your men are followin' us right now?"

"Yes."

"How many?"

"A total of seven," said Debra.

"But don't be discouraged by the number, because those same seven men have taken down entire armies on their own."

"I bet." Heaven's view was laden with doubt.

"All you gotta do is say the word."

Heaven didn't reply. She was calling Pumpkin's phone. Uh-oh.

Chapter 33

The call from Harmoni came while LaShonda and Tony were in the process of fucking. It had been a week now, and a good nut was in high demand. So Harmon's call wasn't answered, besides Teddy P was the only other person that existed during that moment, as he poured from the sound system. By the second call, which came from Harmoni's mama, Lisa, the fuck session was going hard, as Tony pounded into LaShonda, missionary style, and had mama toes curling in pleasure.

But all that came to a sudden halt, when someone began pounding on the front door. Tony tried to ignore it and kept on stroking, but LaShonda wasn't having it and told him to go get the door. Grudgingly, Tony pulled out slowly and stepped into his boxer shorts and stomped his way out of the bedroom for the front door.

A minute later, a team of hooliganz were standing in the living room, with guns drawn, explaining that they were only acting on the orders given by White Boy Ty.

"Where is my son?" Tony demanded.

It was Hollow that stepped up and assured Tony and LaShonda that it was their safety that was of concern. But LaShonda wasn't trying to hear that, and asked to speak with her son.

"Here." Hollow produced the phone to which he hit Jamir's number on speed dial. LaShonda snatched the phone away from him and demanded answers from her son.

"Just do as they say, mama. It's not safe for you and daddy right now, and y'all need to leave the house," said Jamir.

"This shit again, Jay?" LaShonda was angry.

"It's worse this time, mama."

"How worse?"

When he told her what Heaven had just done, his mama's mouth dropped in disbelief. That's all he had to say to convince her that real danger was amiss. So she went and packed up a few much needed things, which she knew she would appreciate where she was going, Tony reentered the bedroom, minutes later, after talking to the hooliganz, to find LaShonda holding his .9mm and he cell phone in her hand, with a dark look in her eyes.

"What is it baby?" He replied, cautiously.

"That was Monica," she said.

"She feels the same way I feel about all his mess, Tony. They're brotha and sista, it just don't make no damn sense."

"Hev doesn't see that shit right now, Shonda. All she knows is her father's death was caused by the very same people she trusted. She hurtin' right now, and the only way to cure that hurt is to—"

"Murder my son? Her own brotha?"

"Baby-" Tony was cut off by the sound of automatic rounds ringing out all around them, as bullets ripped through the walls of the house. Instinctively, Tony dove for his woman and tackled her to the floor, covering her body with his own. LaShonda screamed in fear at the throes of violence erupting by the multiple rounds exploding, as the hooliganz traded round for round with the drive-by car filled with armed Royals outside.

"Tony get off me." LaShonda struggled beneath her husband, as all two hundred twenty pounds of him pinned her down. Tony did not move.

"Baby, c'mon, get up. We gotta go," she cried, fearing the worst and knowing, without a doubt, what just took place would change everything.

Seconds later, Hollow and Lil One entered the room to find her struggling beneath Tony. They knew from the moment they walked through the door that it was over. The hole in the back of his head and the one in his upper back, near his shoulder, was evidence in itself.

"Tony?" LaShonda wept. She had seen the truth in the eyes of the two hooligans, and instead of trying to push him away from her, LaShonda clung to her dead husband.

"C'mon, mama, I gotta get'cha outta here," Hollow said, as he reached for her.

"No," she sobbed.

Hollow looked over at his brother. Then two more hooliganz came into the room and Hollow ordered them to move Tony. Without a thought, they rolled Tony away from on top of her and LaShonda then rolled over on top of him. She buried her face into his still chest and cried sorrowfully.

"What?" Lil One exchanged a look with the others, who looked at him as though he had all the answers.

Sucking his teeth, Hollow bit his bottom lip and took a hold of LaShonda's arm. Then he pulled her up roughly and away from her dead husband.

"Let's go," he demanded. "Now, mama." Hollow pulled her toward the door and out into the hallway, where he felt the tip of LaShonda's gun press into his cheek.

"I said no," she said, as tears spilled from her eyes. "I am not leaving my husband."

"But, what can you do for him now, mama?" Hollow knew if he didn't get her away from that house, their situation was going to get much worse.

"I can't leave him," LaShonda said.

"He's gone though, ma."

"No." LaShonda shook her head solemnly.

"But they could come back again-"

"I'm not running any more, Hollow. I can't. I'm no fuckin' punk bitch," she spazzed out at him, as she pressed the gun deeper into his face. "That little heffa had my husband killed and I want blood for mine," said LaShonda.

"We gon' get blood, ma. I promise you."

"I mean my way, Hollow," she growled. "This ain't Jay's call no more, nor yours, Hollow. What I fuckin' say goes now. You will listen to me, okay?"

"Y-yeah, mama," Hollow agreed.

"Okay. Now take me to her. I want that little bitch's damn head," LaShonda demanded. Then she lowered the gun and shoved Hollow forward. "Let's go."

As he made his way towards the front door with his hooliganz, Hollow gave them the nod that spoke volumes, where LaShonda's authority was concerned.

Jamir was gonna hit the roof when he found out what his mama was about to have them do.

She was scorned. Mama had blood in her eyes.

Chapter 34

Debra Moretti grew up in Vicenza, Italy, on property that had a stream running through it, and multiple acres of woods out back, where her and her three friends could play a number of games. One of them was "Cowboys and Indians," which taught her the value of war. Once they made their own weapons, wooden daggers, slingshots, and even a makeshift stick gun, equipped with rubber band, rock projectiles, until one of her friends lost one eye in the process. Most of her friends were boys and wound up joining the Army.

When Debra turned fifteen, her and her father started fighting a lot, after the death of her mother, a year prior, and she immediately got into trouble around her area and in school. Her father was a drill sergeant, who always kept the family well provided for, but there was tremendous turmoil at home, a lot of drinking, and a lot of physical abuse against her. One morning, things got out of hand and Debra's father hit her like a man. She came back later and shot him dead, with his own gun. Then she ran away from home and never returned for any reason whatsoever.

Years later, she found her way to the United States and made New York her home. Debra was nineteen years old and far from green to her surroundings. She had done her proper home-work on the big city and used its experiences to the best of her ability.

She met Sebastian Kosinski, a carpenter, and he started counseling her. Debra spent many days at his wood shop, carving shit out of wood and talking. That was until the day, months later, when Samuel "Sammy" Moretti walked into the shop, looking for something to purchase for his great-aunt, Rose. That day changed Debra's life forever. Two years later, she found herself married into the Moretti Family, to the nephew of a notorious crime boss and mafia don.

As the years followed, Debra was shown a life that she only thought existed in novels and movies. Then the old man died, making her husband, Sammy, the new don. But with this new found power, a lot of people died, more money was made, and Debra became the primary object to put an end to the madness her husband was creating. She had watched the Moretti family go to war with four other families, and emerge the victor. But by this time, the alphabet boys were involved, and the family was under heavy scrutiny and about to go down, before Marlon intervened. He had warned them of the anticipated sting and convinced Debra and her family to move out, just in the nick of time.

After making sure her and her family were safe, Marlon then played a part in revealing everything he knew that the Feds knew to destroy their whole family. Then Sammy offered up himself as a sacrifice to save his family, and left her in charge of his men and Marlon. He later died in federal custody, leaving Debra to take up the role of matriarch.

She relocated what was left of the family to Chicago, where a cousin of the Moretti family took her in and built a wall of protection around her. After a while, she learned of his disloyalty and personally murdered him, along with his blended family, and then disappeared, without a trace. For the next year or so, Debra survived off her own influence and the provisions that her husband left behind, which she claimed as her own. Then she heard about the matters that were taking place down in the small town, called Quincy, the very same place where Marlon had so proudly said he was from. Debra then contacted Marlon, they met up in South

Georgia, she offered him her help, and then he was murdered.

"I think your father knew he was going to die that night," said Debra to Heaven, as they now occupied the new hideaway that was located out in east Quincy.

"What makes you say that?" Heaven asked.

"Because he wasn't sure if Ced could handle the type of pressure Lyonell was going to apply. He was considering revealing his identity, in hopes that he could prevent what he knew was coming. But before he could do that, Dejah had already sank her claws into him," she said.

Heaven gritted her teeth at that last statement, visualizing what her father's last moment could have been like. She knew Marlon wasn't afraid to die, he would accept his fate with his head high. As far as Ced was concerned, she had cared about him a great deal, but his love was fake. He was just doing his job, a favor for her real father. Heaven was mad at Marlon. His betrayal cut her deeply, as well, but she understood his plight. If he was still alive, she could have definitely made him feel her wrath, while at the same time, loving and appreciating him.

Marlon started all this shit that they were all going through, at the moment. If he would have just kept it real, then maybe none of this would exist.

She wouldn't be queen of the streets. Her brothers would be safe. But all that shit was just wishful thinking, and all Heaven felt from it was anguish and forlorn.

"We have so much more to work towards, Hev," said Debra.

Leaning forward with her hands, Heaven let out an exasperating breath.

"But I see that it's too late to turn back now," Debra added.

Just minutes ago, Heaven had been informed about the deaths of her Royals. Somehow Jamir had managed to get away, with the help of Toby and White Boy Ty. There was no telling where they were now, and it frustrated Heaven that she allowed it to go this far.

Debra's right, thought Heaven. *It's too late to turn back now that the blood has been spilled.*

Jamir was not going to let her get away with what was done. That's why she had her family well-secured in another spot that she knew Rikah knew nothing of. Heaven was smart. She was always prepared for such matters.

"Just make your next move is your best move," said Debra, as she finally rose up to her feet. "And since you refused to accept my offer to help you with this war, I will now take my leave."

"Where are you going?"

"I'll be around," said Debra.

Heaven looked indecisive for a second.

"I'll keep in touch, Hev. But if you do survive this war, just know that my original offer still stands."

"To cure my worries and make me a happy woman?" Heaven replied, with a hint of sarcasm.

The older woman nodded. Then she took her leave, without another word spoken.

When she stepped past the team of Royals guarding the premises outside the house, Debra raised her hand and three of her men suddenly appeared, out of nowhere. Their presence alarmed the Royals, and Debra assured them that all was well. The three armed Italian goons circled around her and escorted Debra toward the curb, where two black SUVs came rolling to a stop before her. The rear passenger door was opened for her and Debra was helped into the back of the lead vehicle.

"Where to, Mrs. Moretti?" asked the driver, who was a big bear of a man behind the wheel.

"Take me back to my hotel suite. I'm exhausted. Thank you, Nicky," she said with a yawn. Then she laid her head back and closed her eyes.

Chapter 35

From a distance, Rikah watched as the two SUVs pulled up, Debra Moretti got inside the first one, and was driven away. After all this happened, Rikah couldn't believe she was still alive to prove to Heaven that she was not to be underestimated. There was a reason she survived this far in the streets, and it had everything to do with her being able to think outside the box.

When Rikah sensed Heaven's intention to kill Redd earlier, she knew there was a possibility that her life would be in danger, as well. Heaven had become absolutely relentless with her murder game, instilling fear in those under her leadership and strengthening her power of authority. Ever since she got her first taste of raw power and blood, Heaven had turned into a monster that couldn't be tamed. The young woman that Rikah had grown to love was now an enemy, who wished death upon her.

Rikah represented the thug life mentality and she knew Heaven was aware of how dangerous she was at that point. When she snuck out of the warehouse earlier, Rikah didn't contact the rest of the HCG crew to warn them. Her mission was to secure the upper hand on Heaven from the Royal Mafia crew as swiftly as she could. Calling her hooligans would only complicate her mission, when Rikah knew that she could handle the situation all by her lonesome. She also knew Debra had her own team, lying in wait at her beck, in case their services were needed, at which time they would respond promptly. She had informed Redd of this and they decided to keep it to themselves. Redd thought it would be best that Debra's hidden team of Italian goons be kept under wraps and pretend that they didn't exist, only to use their presence as a strategic effort to watch discreetly and learn their structure. Keeping them lost on the fact that their presence had been detected would allow them to remain relaxed in their own belief.

Prior to this effort, Rikah had decided to use her recently purchased devices that she'd acquired from the black web. These devices were GPS and listening devices that were advertised to be of high grade, and worth the investment. Good thing Rikah had two of those GPS tracking devices in the car that she planned to use on a potential target. When she snuck out of the building, Rikah rushed to the car to collect the devices and planted them on Heaven's car and one of the backup vehicles.

Heaven had a habit of switching cars, like she does her clothes. Both her backup car and the Wraith were bullet proof, along with the Bentley and one of the SUVs that she also traveled in often. Planting the two tracking devices had to be done swiftly, because they were going to be searching for her soon. Plus, she had to convince the hidden Italian goons that she was acting according to her position as chief enforcer. She took the chance and risk being caught on her game, only to see now that she had done well for herself. Now she knew where Hev was hiding, which was unexpected. Rikah was not supposed to know the new location because, prior to placing the GPS devices, the place did not exist to her. Seeing that Heaven kept this location away from her only made Rikah hungrier for blood.

"You should know better," sang Rikah as she observed her surroundings. There were three Royals posted up outside the house, with another three inside, guarding their queen. If Heaven thought she was well protected, then she had another thing coming.

Knowing just how she was going to handle the situation, Rikah stepped out from the shadows to make her move. For the past half hour, she had maneuvered through the night, putting herself in position, without being spotted by Debra's men nor the Royals. Her effort was about to earn her the upper hand against her opponents.

The silencer screwed to the tip of her pistol would do its job, without the others being the wiser inside the house. The last thing Heaven would expect to see at the moment was her.

Like a muthafuckin' ghost, Rikah would appear. The element of surprise giving her the upper hand.

While the three Royals were guarding the front of the house, Rikah was easing through the shadows from behind the house next door. Then she slipped over, alongside of the house in question, with her gun cocked and ready to lay some shit down. Just several yards away, around the corner, were Brianna, Quanda and Milk Shake, three women that Rikah had mad love for. She knew she had to shut her emotions off in order to survive this. She had to be thorough and deadly, no room for mistakes, or else she would surely die tonight.

Just when she was about to spin the corner on them bitches and gun them down, Rikah was stopped by the sudden arrival of a dark sedan, pulling up and stopping outside of the house. From her vantage point, she watched with growing anticipation. The passenger doors opened and three people exited the car. One of them Rikah knew, without a shadow of doubt. She would know them from anywhere, and seeing them now made her look in total bewilderment and shock.

It was the element of surprise for her.

"What the fuck?" whispered Rikah, as she watched none other than Marlon approach the front door of the house.

This was some freaky shit. He was supposed to be dead...

Again.

Chapter 36

Dejah was working on her third set of sit-ups, when she heard Mookie gasp in surprise. She sat up and looked across the cell at her. Mookie looked back at her and Dejah saw the open shock mixed with fear on her face. Mookie was on the phone with her people, when the notification came that an incoming video call was in progress. When she switched over to the video call Mookie got the shock of her life.

"The fuck is wrong wit' you?" Asked Dejah.

Suddenly, Mookie's eyes watered up with tears and that shit didn't settle well with Dejah. She got up from where she was using the bottom of the cell door to support her sit-ups. When she made her way over to her cellmate, Mookie was shaking her head sadly.

"What you lookin' at, Mook?"

"You don't wanna see this," said Mookie cautiously.

Dejah frowned.

"Gimme the jack, Mookie, and miss me wit' all that shit," she said with her hand extended.

The door window was covered with a thick, dark blanket to keep the others out of their business. The guards were a little lenient with them on the night shift. They would just keep it moving when they saw the window covered, expecting nothing more than their privacy being honored, while using the bathroom or indulging in sexual activities.

Reluctantly, Mookie handed over the cellphone and Dejah, looking down at the screen to inspect what was there, gasped and reeled back instantly, in absolute horror at what lied before her eyes. It was a short video of Redd being shot in the head, as the shooter's identity was distorted in a haze of interference to prevent physical identification. But Dejah knew only a chosen few people had her number, and one of them being Heaven, who was close to Redd and surprisingly bold enough to murder her without repercussion.

Seeing the video shook Dejah to the core. She had to sit down to gather her bearings, because what was about to transpire would no doubt determine how she would respond.

"Why Redd, though?" muttered Mookie.

There was no answer from Dejah, because she didn't have one to offer. She forced her eye water to remain at bay, and made the call that would change everything.

She called Heaven.

"I was wondering when you were gon' call, Dej," said Heaven in a very cold tone of voice. "Did you like the movie that I sent you?"

"Why, Hev?" Dejah closed her eyes.

"You know you're the next one in line, but the last person I expected to cross me."

"Cross you how, Hev? What the fuck did I do?" Dejah felt Mookie's hand on her leg, and she looked down to see the expression in her eyes.

"How bout I show you instead, Dej?"

When the phone vibrated, Dejah looked down to see there was another video being sent to her phone. Heaven was being very adamant about proving how she felt and where her sudden cruel intentions were derived from. Dejah was almost scared to view the video attachment but opened up the link anyway.

It was a video of Marlon being led out of the bar, some time ago, while in her company. It showed how he was forced into a truck and driven away. As she watched this video, Dejah thought back to that night. The last moments of Marlon's life before she killed him were so vivid in her mind that she could still hear the gunshot that finally took him out of his misery.

That was when the tears came. Dejah was being confronted for her actions and Heaven was not going to have it any other way, except for death as a payment for her actions.

"You did this to me," Heaven said to her.

"I was only protecting you," said Dejah.

"Bitch, protectin' me how?" Heaven snapped. "And you know how I felt about losing my father. You didn't even care about how that shit would affect me and my life. No. You thought I'd never find out what you did, Dej. You killed my father and tried to hide it from me."

"He would have only caused you more hurt, Hev. I didn't want you to go through that shit again."

"You never gave me the opportunity to decide that, Dejah."

Dejah had no reply to that.

"Now the whole squad is gonna to pay for this," said Heaven.

"What do you mean by that? What are you saying, Hev?" said Dejah with a speeding heart rate.

If what Heaven was insinuating to her was really her intentions, then Dejah knew that she was in a whole world of trouble.

Heaven's next words were something she never would have expected to ever hear from her in a million years.

"The whole Hooliganz Crime Gang has to pay for participating in my father's death," said Heaven in obvious contempt.

"You can't be serious," said Dejah.

"I'm very serious, Dej. And Jay was my first victim. Too bad he got away, though. But after tonight, the existence of Hooliganz Crime Gang will be destroyed."

"You can't do this, Heaven."

"It's already done."

"What about Shamar, then, Hev? Huh?"

"What about him?" She retorted.

Dejah dropped her head and thought about how she should choose her next words.

"I know, Hev." she replied.

"You know what?"

"About you and Mar."

"You don't know shit, Dejah. But don't worry, I'ma see that you get dealt wit' accordingly."

"Even your own daughter's real true father, too? Yeah. Like I said, I know, Hev. I know Shamar is Aliyah's father and not LJ. Now, my question to you is, would you do that to your own daughter?" Dejah replied.

For a long moment there was no reply from Heaven. She had hit a very tender spot that Heaven left her with no other choice but to recall her actions.

Then the phone disconnected.

Heaven was gone.

"I can't believe this shit," Dejah groaned loudly, and forced herself not to slam the phone to the floor.

Mookie had heard enough to know that shit was about to get very drastic for them. With Heavens new status and power, it was going to be difficult to get from under the heavy blow she was about to deliver.

"Is it really true, Dejah?" Mookie asked.

"What?"

"That Shamar is Hev's baby daddy?"

The question made Dejah seethe with disdain.

"Of all the other serious shit we got goin' on, you ask me some stupid shit like that?"

Mookie just stared at her quietly.

"Yeah, Mook," said Dejah. "It's true. Hev cheated on LJ wit' her own brotha and had baby by him."

All Mookie could do was shake her head as she thought, *if it ain't one thing it's another.*

Chapter 37

They were three deep in an unmarked car, when they turned onto Key Street and saw all the police lights flashing in the night. White Boy Ty brought the car to a halt immediately. From the back seat, Toby looked up at Jamir and already knew what was going through his head at that moment. Then, before anyone could say anything, Jamir was out of the car and rushing towards his house, where the crime scene was taking place.

"Shit." Toby cussed under her breath and jumped out of the car to go after him.

As he ran towards his house, the only thing Jamir could think about was his mama and Tony. Police cars and other emergency vehicles lined the stretch of road to Jamir's childhood home, and a yellow police tape barrier stretched across the little sliver of grass in front of the house. Uniformed officers came and went through the front door. Jamir had no regard for the yellow tape and ran right through it for the front door. But before he could make it to the door, he was grabbed by two officers, who struggled him to the ground.

When she saw that, Toby rushed in and shoved one of the cops away from Jamir. When a third cop advanced on her, Toby punched him in the neck and laid his fat ass out on his back.

"No. Stop it. No, no, no!" Out of nowhere came the one and only Detective Angie Galloway, shoving her way through the clusters of cops, who suddenly abandoned the primary task to assist their fellow officers.

"Maddox, back off. I got this. I got it. Get your sergeant, Blaire." she directed her attention to the big white cop, who Toby had squared up with. "I'll handle these two. They're my people."

"Lemme go. Get off me, cracka." Jamir was resisting beneath the cop, who had his knee in his back. Toby was inching closer so she could kick the white cop dead in his fucking' face and put hands on him.

Angie saw this and laid a hand on Toby's arm. Then she moved over to order the cop to release Jamir at once.

"This is his home," she said. "I got it."

"But there's a crime scene here, Lieutenant?" he replied.

"You think I don't fuckin' know that, Earl?" said Angie, with a dark scowl on her face. Then she turned her attention to Jamir.

"Jay you gon' have to calm down and humble yourself. If you don't, then you're gonna force my and I don't wanna make them detain you."

"Lemme go," Jamir snarled up at the cop.

"Do we have an understanding, Jay?" Asked Angie.

Tears were spilling from Jamir's eyes at that moment. Upon seeing this, Toby ignored the detectives warning and stepped over to intervene, before she was stopped again.

"I'm here," said Kiara, who suddenly appeared out of nowhere and helped Jamir up from the ground. All it took was that look she gave the white cop restraining Jamir and he let him go immediately.

Jamir got to his feet, and without a word, he made his way to the front door of the house. A couple of officers standing nearby wanted so badly to stop him, but it appeared that Angie held the higher authority over them.

"I'll go wit' him," said Detective Galloway to her cousin.

Kiara, glaring at her coldly, nodded her head.

In the foyer of the house Jamir, halted instantly, as if he was trying to build up the courage to go further. That's when Angie appeared behind him, along with two of her officers, who were ready to act at her slightest whim.

"Jay?" she whispered to him.

He looked back at her with a deranged look in his weary eyes.

"I don't think it's wise to go in there and witness what happened, son," she told him.

"I wanna see my mama," he said slowly.

"Baby, your mama ain't in this house."

The look of surprise on his face was evident.

"It's Tony," Angie replied.

At hearing those words, Jamir dropped his head, as a fresh stream of tears fell from his eyes. He fought the losing battle to calm himself down, and then Angie opened out her arms to him. She had known him since he was born, and watched Jamir grow up fast. He and his brothers and Heaven had given her pure hell over the years, but she always found a way to be there for them, when all else failed. But at that very moment, Angie felt partially guilty for what was transpiring between her and him. She wished there was a way that she could shield him from truth of the matter.

"Where is my mama?" he asked. Jamir's fists were clenched tightly, as if he was ready to fight.

"We don't know," said Angie.

Jamir looked in the direction where he now knew Tony lay dead to this world. He stood there for long moment, thinking of how much he wanted to find Heaven now and rip her fuckin' head off. But first, he needed to find his mama and make sure she was okay.

"I'ma need to ask you some questions, Jay, to try and figure out who did this mess," said Detective Galloway.

"I already know who," Jamir replied, before he realized the words had left his mouth.

"Who? Who did this to your family?"

With the shake of his head, Jamir brushed past her, headed back outside with that cold look in his eyes.

"Jay," she called out after him.

He just kept right on walking. Jamir only had two things on his mind at that point, his mama and killing Heaven.

Back outside, Kiara and Toby fell in step alongside of him, as he made his way across the street to Heaven's old home. Although he knew no one was there, he still made his way around to the back, where he kicked in the backdoor to gain entrance.

"What's going on?" Kiara asked Toby at the backdoor of Monica's house, scared to follow Jamir inside.

Toby said, "Go home, Aunt Kay."

"Is it Hev that's behind all this mess?"

"Go home."

And just when Kiara was about to respond, a shot rang out inside the house. With the quickness, Toby drew her gun and rushed inside the house. Kiara was right behind her and what they saw next was totally unexpected.

Then more shots rang out. And then total chaos.

Chapter 38

During that very same moment, LaShonda stood outside Heaven's mini mansion and watched as it burned. Her and the four hooliganz, who were now under her control, had searched the big house and found no one inside. So she made them set the house on fire, because if anyone was in their hiding in some secret hidden place, they would either burn to death or come out and still die in the process.

"We good," said LaShonda, clutching the pistol in her hand and making her way back to the SUV, where Hollow, who couldn't believe he was out there thuggin' with the mother of his superior, opened the door for her to get inside.

Also present was Zamon, Lil One and Erick. They all got into the SUV and the car they came in.

It was decided that Heaven had gotten to her family before anyone else could. By now, they were probably nowhere in the county, for fear of being detected and retaliated against. LaShonda could think of a few more places that Anya and Monica would feel safer under such circumstances. She would go and see if that was where they had gone.

Before LaShonda could inform Hollow where she wanted to go next, Lil One's cell phone rang. At the sound of the ringing phone, LaShonda instinctively reached for her own phone, which was not in her possession. She had left it back at the house, where Tony now lay dead and cold to the touch.

"What's up, Bush Boy?" Answered Lil One.

In the back seat, next to Zamon, who had sparked up a blunt, its potent smoke teasing her senses, LaShonda reached over and took blunt away for him.

"Mannn," Zamon whined, as LaShonda took a pull from it.

"What? Are you for real?" Lil One blurted out suddenly.

LaShonda said, "For real about what, Lil One?"

Right then, Zamon's cell phone sounded off and he saw that it was AV calling him.

For some reason, LaShonda sensed something very disturbing was happening at that moment. She could tell by the way Lil One was responding to his call that whoever it was on the other end was telling him something worrisome. Then Zamon began to get agitated and started yelling into his own phone and cussing like a madman.

Something serious was going down.

The hooliganz sounded scared about something.

"Can somebody please tell me what the fuck is going on?" Said LaShonda, as the blunt sizzled in her hand.

"Hev don' snapped again," said Lil One, hanging up with Bush Boy, seconds later.

"What she don' did now?"

"She don' sent her squad after all the families of everybody in the crew. Bush Boy's old boy just got killed. Lil Eddie don' got caught slippin', tryna get his baby mama and his little son somewhere safe. They shot the car up and killed everybody in the car. Peanut and Twan caught three of them Royal bitches in traffic, and they lit that muthafucka up. It's crazy out here," said Lil One with a deep sigh.

Hitting the blunt again, LaShonda nodded her head and willed herself to remain cool.

"Let's get back to Quincy-" she was interrupted by the sound of Lil One's phone sounding off, once again.

When he answered the phone, he spoke only a few words. Then he turned in his seat to offer LaShonda the phone next.

She hesitated for a second, then cast caution aside an accepted the phone.

"Who is this?" She demanded.

"It's me," said Heaven.

Instant hate filled LaShonda's heart, at that moment. "Bitch you got some nerve," she hissed venomously. "Where the fuck you at? I wanna see your ass, face to face."

"You wanna kill me, right?" Heaven replied.

LaShonda had to catch herself before she exploded.

"Anyway, you can get in line with the rest of 'em. But yeah, what I wanna know is this, why didn't you tell me that you and my father were lovers?"

"What?"

"You heard what I said."

Stunned by her question, LaShonda closed her eyes for a moment and dwelled on the situation.

"Jay is his son, too," added Heaven. "You knew this the whole time and failed to say anything about it. Now my brotha don' played a part in his murder," she said.

"He did no such thang, you little bitch."

"Why the fuck you think I'm doing what I'm doing? Jay is my real brotha and you hid that from us. Now you will pay for that shit, too," Heaven said.

"Fuck you!" LaShonda had tears in her eyes. "I'll see you when I see you. Until then, I'ma make you wish you never fucked wit' me and my family." With that being said, she disconnected the call and turned her gaze on Hollow. "Take me straight to Lake Skillet," she said.

"What's there?" He asked.

After a brief moment, LaShonda said, "Her heart."

TO BE CONTINUED...

COMING NEXT:

LAND OF DA HOOLIGANZ PT. III
AGAINST ALL ODDS

BY: Ira L. Bunion
BKA
IRA B.

ON POINT CREATIONS

Lock Down Publications and Ca$h Presents
Assisted Publishing Packages

BASIC PACKAGE	UPGRADED PACKAGE
$499	$800
Editing	Typing
Cover Design	Editing
Formatting	Cover Design
	Formatting
ADVANCE PACKAGE	**LDP SUPREME PACKAGE**
$1,200	$1,500
Typing	Typing
Editing	Editing
Cover Design	Cover Design
Formatting	Formatting
Copyright registration	Copyright registration
Proofreading	Proofreading
Upload book to Amazon	Set up Amazon account
	Upload book to Amazon
	Advertise on LDP, Amazon and
	Facebook Page

***Other services available upon request.
Additional charges may apply

Lock Down Publications
P.O. Box 944
Stockbridge, GA 30281-9998
Phone: 470 303-9761

Submission Guideline

Submit the first three chapters of your completed manuscript to ldpsubmissions@gmail.com. In the subject line add **Your Book's Title**. The manuscript must be in a Word Doc file and sent as an attachment. Document should be in Times New Roman, double spaced, and in size 12 font. Also, provide your synopsis and full contact information. If sending multiple submissions, they must each be in a separate email.

Have a story but no way to send it electronically? You can still submit to LDP/Ca$h Presents. Send in the first three chapters, written or typed, of your completed manuscript to:

LDP: Submissions Dept
P.O. Box 944
Stockbridge, GA 30281-9998

DO NOT send original manuscript. Must be a duplicate.
Provide your synopsis and a cover letter containing your full contact information.

Thanks for considering LDP and Ca$h Presents.

NEW RELEASES

BLOODLINE OF A SAVAGE 1&2
THESE VICIOUS STREETS
RELENTLESS GOON
RELENTLESS GOON 2
BY PRINCE A. TAUHID

THE BUTTERFLY MAFIA 1-3
BY FUMIYA PAYNE

A THUG'S STREET PRINCESS 1&2
BY MEESHA

CITY OF SMOKE 2
BY MOLOTTI

STEPPERS 1,2&3
BY KING RIO

THE LANE 1&2
BY KEN-KEN SPENCE

THUG OF SPADES 1&2
LOVE IN THE TRENCHES 2
BY COREY ROBINSON

TIL DEATH 3
BY ARYANNA

THE BIRTH OF A GANGSTER 4
BY DELMONT PLAYER

LAND OF THE HOOLIGANZ 2 | IRA B

PRODUCT OF THE STREETS 1&2
BY DEMOND "MONEY" ANDERSON

NO TIME FOR ERROR
BY KEESE

MONEY HUNGRY DEMONS
BY TRANAY ADAMS

Coming Soon from Lock Down Publications/Ca$h Presents

IF YOU CROSS ME ONCE 6
ANGEL V
By Anthony Fields

IMMA DIE BOUT MINE 4&5
By Aryanna

A THUGS STREET PRINCESS 3
By Meesha

PRODUCT OF THE STREETS 3
By Demond Money Anderson

CORNER BOYS
By Corey Robinson

SON OF A DOPE FIEND 4
By Renta

THE MURDER QUEENS 6&7
By Michael Gallon

CITY OF SMOKE 3
By Molotti

BETRAYAL OF A G
By Ray Vinci

CONFESSIONS OF A DOPE BOY
By Nicholas Lock

THA TAKEOVER
By Keith Chandler

Available Now

RESTRAINING ORDER 1 & 2
By **CA$H & Coffee**

LOVE KNOWS NO BOUNDARIES 1-3
By **Coffee**

RAISED AS A GOON I, II, III & IV
BRED BY THE SLUMS I, II, III
BLAST FOR ME I & II
ROTTEN TO THE CORE I II III
A BRONX TALE I, II, III
DUFFLE BAG CARTEL I II III IV V VI
HEARTLESS GOON I II III IV V
A SAVAGE DOPEBOY I II
DRUG LORDS I II III
CUTTHROAT MAFIA I II
KING OF THE TRENCHES
By **Ghost**

LAY IT DOWN I & II
LAST OF A DYING BREED I II
BLOOD STAINS OF A SHOTTA I & II III
By **Jamaica**

LOYAL TO THE GAME I II III
LIFE OF SIN I, II III
By **TJ & Jelissa**

IF LOVING HIM IS WRONG…I & II
LOVE ME EVEN WHEN IT HURTS I II III
By **Jelissa**

BLOODY COMMAS I & II
SKI MASK CARTEL I, II & III
KING OF NEW YORK I II, III IV V
RISE TO POWER I II III
COKE KINGS I II III IV V
BORN HEARTLESS I II III IV
KING OF THE TRAP I II
By **T.J. Edwards**

WHEN THE STREETS CLAP BACK I & II III
THE HEART OF A SAVAGE I II III IV
MONEY MAFIA I II
LOYAL TO THE SOIL I II III
By **Jibril Williams**

A DISTINGUISHED THUG STOLE MY HEART I II &
III
LOVE SHOULDN'T HURT I II III IV
RENEGADE BOYS 1-4
PAID IN KARMA 1-3
SAVAGE STORMS 1-3
AN UNFORESEEN LOVE 1-3
BABY, I'M WINTERTIME COLD 1-3
A THUG'S STREET PRINCESS 1&2
By **Meesha**

A GANGSTER'S CODE 1-3
A GANGSTER'S SYN 1-3
THE SAVAGE LIFE 1-3
CHAINED TO THE STREETS 1-3
BLOOD ON THE MONEY 1-3
A GANGSTA'S PAIN 1-3
BEAUTIFUL LIES AND UGLY TRUTHS
CHURCH IN THESE STREETS
By **J-Blunt**

PUSH IT TO THE LIMIT
By **Bre' Hayes**

BLOOD OF A BOSS 1-5
SHADOWS OF THE GAME
TRAP BASTARD
By **Askari**

THE STREETS BLEED MURDER 1-3
THE HEART OF A GANGSTA 1-3
By **Jerry Jackson**

CUM FOR ME 1-8
An LDP Erotica Collaboration

BRIDE OF A HUSTLA 1-3
THE FETTI GIRLS 1-3
CORRUPTED BY A GANGSTA 1-4
BLINDED BY HIS LOVE
THE PRICE YOU PAY FOR LOVE 1-3
DOPE GIRL MAGIC 1-3
By **Destiny Skai**

WHEN A GOOD GIRL GOES BAD
By **Adrienne**

A KINGPIN'S AMBITION
A KINGPIN'S AMBITION II
I MURDER FOR THE DOUGH
By **Ambitious**

THE COST OF LOYALTY 1-3
By **Kweli**

A GANGSTER'S REVENGE 1-4
THE BOSS MAN'S DAUGHTERS 1-5
A SAVAGE LOVE 1&2
BAE BELONGS TO ME 1&2
A HUSTLER'S DECEIT 1-3
WHAT BAD BITCHES DO 1-3
SOUL OF A MONSTER 1-3
KILL ZONE
A DOPE BOY'S QUEEN 1-3
TIL DEATH 1-3
IMMA DIE BOUT MINE 1-3
By **Aryanna**

TRUE SAVAGE 1-7
DOPE BOY MAGIC 1-3
MIDNIGHT CARTEL 1-3
CITY OF KINGZ 1&2
NIGHTMARE ON SILENT AVE
THE PLUG OF LIL MEXICO 1&2
CLASSIC CITY
By **Chris Green**

A DOPEBOY'S PRAYER
By **Eddie "Wolf" Lee**

THE KING CARTEL 1-3
By **Frank Gresham**

THESE NIGGAS AIN'T LOYAL 1-3
By **Nikki Tee**

GANGSTA SHYT 1-3
By **CATO**

THE ULTIMATE BETRAYAL
By **Phoenix**

BOSS'N UP 1-3
By **Royal Nicole**

I LOVE YOU TO DEATH
By **Destiny J**

I RIDE FOR MY HITTA
I STILL RIDE FOR MY HITTA
By **Misty Holt**

LOVE & CHASIN' PAPER
By **Qay Crockett**

TO DIE IN VAIN
SINS OF A HUSTLA
By **ASAD**

BROOKLYN HUSTLAZ
By **Boogsy Morina**

BROOKLYN ON LOCK 1 & 2
By **Sonovia**

GANGSTA CITY
By **Teddy Duke**

A DRUG KING AND HIS DIAMOND 1-3
A DOPEMAN'S RICHES
HER MAN, MINE'S TOO 1&2
CASH MONEY HO'S
THE WIFEY I USED TO BE 1&2
PRETTY GIRLS DO NASTY THINGS
By **Nicole Goosby**

LIPSTICK KILLAH 1-3
CRIME OF PASSION 1-3
FRIEND OR FOE 1-3
By **Mimi**

TRAPHOUSE KING 1-3
KINGPIN KILLAZ 1-3
STREET KINGS 1&2
PAID IN BLOOD 1&2
CARTEL KILLAZ 1-3
DOPE GODS 1&2
By **Hood Rich**

STEADY MOBBN' 1-3
THE STREETS STAINED MY SOUL 1-3
By **Marcellus Allen**

WHO SHOT YA 1-3
SON OF A DOPE FIEND 1-3
HEAVEN GOT A GHETTO 1&2
SKI MASK MONEY 1&2
By **Renta**

GORILLAZ IN THE BAY 1-4
TEARS OF A GANGSTA 1/&2
3X KRAZY 1&2
STRAIGHT BEAST MODE 1&2
By **DE'KARI**

TRIGGADALE 1-3
MURDA WAS THE CASE 1-3
By **Elijah R. Freeman**

THE STREETS ARE CALLING
By **Duquie Wilson**

SLAUGHTER GANG 1-3
RUTHLESS HEART 1-3
By **Willie Slaughter**

GOD BLESS THE TRAPPERS 1-3
THESE SCANDALOUS STREETS 1-3
FEAR MY GANGSTA 1-5
THESE STREETS DON'T LOVE NOBODY 1-2
BURY ME A G 1-5
A GANGSTA'S EMPIRE 1-4
THE DOPEMAN'S BODYGAURD 1&2
THE REALEST KILLAZ 1-3
THE LAST OF THE OGS 1-3
By **Tranay Adams**

MARRIED TO A BOSS 1-3
By **Destiny Skai & Chris Green**

KINGZ OF THE GAME 1-7
CRIME BOSS 1-3
By **Playa Ray**

FUK SHYT
By **Blakk Diamond**

DON'T F#CK WITH MY HEART 1&2
By **Linnea**

ADDICTED TO THE DRAMA 1-3
IN THE ARM OF HIS BOSS
By **Jamila**

LOYALTY AIN'T PROMISED 1&2
By **Keith Williams**

YAYO 1-4
A SHOOTER'S AMBITION 1&2
BRED IN THE GAME
By **S. Allen**

TRAP GOD 1-3
RICH $AVAGE 1-3
MONEY IN THE GRAVE 1-3
CARTEL MONEY
By **Martell Troublesome Bolden**

FOREVER GANGSTA 1&2
GLOCKS ON SATIN SHEETS 1&2
By **Adrian Dulan**

TOE TAGZ 1-4
LEVELS TO THIS SHYT 1&2
IT'S JUST ME AND YOU
By **Ah'Million**

KINGPIN DREAMS 1-3
RAN OFF ON DA PLUG
By **Paper Boi Rari**

CONFESSIONS OF A GANGSTA 1-4
CONFESSIONS OF A JACKBOY 1-3
CONFESSIONS OF A HITMAN
By **Nicholas Lock**

I'M NOTHING WITHOUT HIS LOVE
SINS OF A THUG
TO THE THUG I LOVED BEFORE
A GANGSTA SAVED XMAS
IN A HUSTLER I TRUST
By **Monet Dragun**

QUIET MONEY 1-3
THUG LIFE 1-3
EXTENDED CLIP 1&2
A GANGSTA'S PARADISE
By **Trai'Quan**

CAUGHT UP IN THE LIFE 1-3
THE STREETS NEVER LET GO 1-3
By **Robert Baptiste**

NEW TO THE GAME 1-3
MONEY, MURDER & MEMORIES 1-3
By **Malik D. Rice**

CREAM 2-3
THE STREETS WILL TALK
By **Yolanda Moore**

LIFE OF A SAVAGE 1-4
A GANGSTA'S QUR'AN 1-4
MURDA SEASON 1-3
GANGLAND CARTEL 1-3
CHI'RAQ GANGSTAS 1-4
KILLERS ON ELM STREET 1-3
JACK BOYZ N DA BRONX 1-3
A DOPEBOY'S DREAM 1-3
JACK BOYS VS DOPE BOYS 1-3
COKE GIRLZ
COKE BOYS
SOSA GANG 1&2
BRONX SAVAGES
BODYMORE KINGPINS
BLOOD OF A GOON
By **Romell Tukes**

THE STREETS MADE ME 1-3
By **Larry D. Wright**

CONCRETE KILLA 1-3
VICIOUS LOYALTY 1-3
By **Kingpen**

THE ULTIMATE SACRIFICE 1-6
KHADIFI
IF YOU CROSS ME ONCE 1-3
ANGEL 1-4
IN THE BLINK OF AN EYE
By **Anthony Fields**

THE LIFE OF A HOOD STAR
By **Ca$h & Rashia Wilson**

THE STREETS WILL NEVER CLOSE 1-3
By **K'ajji**

NIGHTMARES OF A HUSTLA 1-3
By **King Dream**

HARD AND RUTHLESS 1&2
MOB TOWN 251
THE BILLIONAIRE BENTLEYS 1-3
REAL G'S MOVE IN SILENCE
By **Von Diesel**

GHOST MOB
By **Stilloan Robinson**

MOB TIES 1-6
SOUL OF A HUSTLER, HEART OF A KILLER 1-3
GORILLAZ IN THE TRENCHES
By **SayNoMore**

BODYMORE MURDERLAND 1-3
THE BIRTH OF A GANGSTER 1-4
By **Delmont Player**

FOR THE LOVE OF A BOSS 1&2
By **C. D. Blue**

KILLA KOUNTY 1-5
By **Khufu**

MOBBED UP 1-4
THE BRICK MAN 1-5
THE COCAINE PRINCESS 1-10
STEPPERS 1-3
SUPER GREMLIN 1-4
By **King Rio**

MONEY GAME 1&2
By **Smoove Dolla**

A GANGSTA'S KARMA 1-4
By **FLAME**

KING OF THE TRENCHES 1-3
By **GHOST & TRANAY ADAMS**

QUEEN OF THE ZOO 1&2
By **Black Migo**

GRIMEY WAYS 1-3
By **Ray Vinci**

XMAS WITH AN ATL SHOOTER
By **Ca$h & Destiny Skai**

LAND OF THE HOOLIGANZ 2 | IRA B

KING KILLA 1&2
By **Vincent "Vitto" Holloway**

BETRAYAL OF A THUG 1&2
By **Fre$h**

THE MURDER QUEENS 1-5
By **Michael Gallon**

FOR THE LOVE OF BLOOD 1-4
By **Jamel Mitchell**

HOOD CONSIGLIERE 1&2
NO TIME FOR ERROR
By **Keese**

PROTÉGÉ OF A LEGEND 1&2
LOVE IN THE TRENCHES 1&2
By **Corey Robinson**

BORN IN THE GRAVE 1-3
CRIME PAYS
By **Self Made Tay**

MOAN IN MY MOUTH
By **XTASY**

TORN BETWEEN A GANGSTER AND A GENTLEMAN
By **J-BLUNT & Miss Kim**

LOYALTY IS EVERYTHING 1-3
CITY OF SMOKE 1&2
By **Molotti**

HERE TODAY GONE TOMORROW 1&2
By **Fly Rock**

WOMEN LIE MEN LIE 1-4
FIFTY SHADES OF SNOW 1-3
STACK BEFORE YOU SPLURGE
GIRLS FALL LIKE DOMINOES
NAÏVE TO THE STREETS
By **ROY MILLIGAN**

PILLOW PRINCESS
By **S. Hawkins**

THE BUTTERFLY MAFIA 1-3
SALUTE MY SAVAGERY 1&2
By **Fumiya Payne**

THE LANE 1&2
By Ken-Ken Spence

THE PUSSY TRAP 1-5
By **Nene Capri**

DIRTY DNA
By **Blaque**

SANCTIFIED AND HORNY
by **XTASY**

BOOKS BY LDP'S CEO, CA$H

TRUST IN NO MAN
TRUST IN NO MAN 2
TRUST IN NO MAN 3
BONDED BY BLOOD
SHORTY GOT A THUG
THUGS CRY
THUGS CRY 2
THUGS CRY 3
TRUST NO BITCH
TRUST NO BITCH 2
TRUST NO BITCH 3
TIL MY CASKET DROPS
RESTRAINING ORDER
RESTRAINING ORDER 2
IN LOVE WITH A CONVICT
LIFE OF A HOOD STAR
XMAS WITH AN ATL SHOOTER

www.ingramcontent.com/pod-product-compliance
Lightning Source LLC
Chambersburg PA
CBHW070519260626
47161CB00004B/1592